## "Who do you think you are?"

Suddenly Jess was infuriated. "Just because Dick was nice to me and showed me Singapore. I thought you were an advocate of experience, Mr. Thorpe!"

Derek's grip on her arms tightened and Jess barely stopped from gasping aloud at the pain. "Let me go, " she cried. But he seemed not to hear, and then slowly, with a smile terrible to see, he bent and took her lips. . . .

It was sometime before he released her and when he did Jess found herself clinging to him. "If it's experience you want," Thorpe said with a harsh mocking smile, "you must come to the master."

---

**NORA POWERS**
taught English at the college level while working on her Ph.D. She now devotes her time to writing novels and says, "I write every day regularly, like I eat and sleep. It's almost that necessary for me."

Dear Reader:

Silhouette Romances is an exciting new publishing venture. We will be presenting the very finest writers of contemporary romantic fiction as well as outstanding new talent in this field. It is our hope that our stories, our heroes and our heroines will give you, the reader, all you want from romantic fiction.

Also, *you* play an important part in our future plans for Silhouette Romances. We welcome any suggestions or comments on our books and I invite you to write to us at the address below.

So, enjoy this book and all the wonderful romances from Silhouette. They're for *you!*

Karen Solem
Editor-in-Chief
Silhouette Books
P. O. Box 769
New York, N.Y. 10019

# NORA POWERS
# Affairs of the Heart

*Silhouette* *Romance*

Published by Silhouette Books New York

**America's Publisher of Contemporary Romance**

Other Silhouette Romances by Nora Powers

*Design for Love*

SILHOUETTE BOOKS, a Simon & Schuster Division of
GULF & WESTERN CORPORATION
1230 Avenue of the Americas, New York, N.Y. 10020

Copyright © 1980 by Silhouette Books

Distributed by Pocket Books

ISBN: 0-671-57003-X

First Silhouette printing May, 1980

10 9 8 7 6 5

America's Publisher of Contemporary Romance

Printed in the U.S.A.

# Affairs
of the Heart

# Chapter 1

Jess Stanton looked eagerly out the window as the big 747 approached Singapore International Airport. As the great plane drew closer the dot that had been the island grew larger. In a series of concentric circles the city spread out before her eyes. At its heart was the muted gray of civilization—tall skyscrapers to rival any in American cities. Around these could be seen strips of lush green vegetation, land which the city proper had not yet reached. And finally the whole was surrounded by the emerald green of the sea. In one place that green seemed dimmer and Jess followed the course of the Singapore River as it wound from the harbor inland. A rather murky brown, its edges seemed to be covered with little brown boats, sampans, Jess supposed, thinking with a smile that they did look like little water bugs, as the guidebook said.

She squirmed anxiously in her seat. The city certainly looked intriguing. She was eager to see it. She forced herself to sit back and relax. What a windfall this assignment had been, especially for a girl from the Montana hills who had not yet made her name well known in photographic circles.

Jess rummaged through her bag and pulled out the letter for the hundredth time. Many readings had left it somewhat the worse for wear, but the expensive quality of the stationery was still quite evident. How very concise this Derek Thorpe was.

Dear Stanton

I have seen your latest spread in *National Wildlife*. I'll give you $20,000 for a summer's work. Enclosed is your ticket to Singapore. You'll be met at customs. We leave for Sarawak and Sabah on July 2nd. Bring anything special. Regular supplies here.

Derek Thorpe

Mr. Thorpe had evidently not considered that she might refuse his offer. And he was right, Jess thought with a wry smile. Certainly, proud as she was of them, none of her nature spreads had earned her a figure like that. This was her big chance, she thought, trying to calm the butterflies that were flitting in her stomach. Derek Thorpe obviously had money—and power. The photos from this trip into the jungle would be her passport to the big time.

She rubbed wearily at her eyes. After all, she had traveled halfway around the world. Excitement had kept her awake when she should have been sleeping and eventually jet lag would take its toll. But none of that mattered at the moment. She was actually approaching Singapore.

Folding up the precious letter, she returned it to her purse and took out a comb. She ran the comb through her unruly red curls and sighed. The first thing she wanted in Singapore was a bath!

Then the landing signs flashed on and she fastened her seat belt and put the comb away. *Well,* she thought, *Singapore, here I come.*

Sometime later a tired Jess stood surrounded by her baggage. There was quite a lot of it, far too much for her to be lugging around, she thought with rising irritation. Just where was the high and mighty Mr.

Thorpe? She had expected to be met before now, but no one had approached her.

She sighed and bit her bottom lip. She was used to hard work and the wilderness, but the trip had been very tiring for her. She could feel her legs begin to tremble with weariness. One of her large cases was quite sturdy and she sat down on it while she considered her situation. She could go to a phone booth and call Thorpe. He must be in the book. And yet surely the man would be here. A ticket to Singapore cost quite a bit of money.

As she debated a crisp voice with a British accent came over the loudspeakers. "J. Stanton, Mr. J. Stanton, please report to the Northwest Orient desk."

Jess, who had half risen from her case, smiled in amusement. What a small world it was. Two J. Stantons arriving in Singapore at the same time and on Northwest Orient planes.

She occupied herself with surveying the crowd as it moved around her. What a diversity of people. Many Europeans seemed to be entering the city, but there were also many oriental people. Chinese girls in their traditional high-necked, side-slitted cheongsams moved gracefully along. Indian women in silken saris, their nose rings glittering, followed their turbanned husbands.

The people looked fascinating and Jess wished to get this worrisome waiting over so she could begin to see the city. Again the brisk British voice came over the loudspeaker. "J. Stanton, Mr. Jess Stanton. Please call the Northwest Orient desk."

*Mr.* Jess Stanton! Jess was startled. That was too much of a coincidence. Someone had made a mistake. She rose and headed for the phone. Moments later she spotted the man she had spoken to as he came toward her closely followed by a customs official. He was as he had described himself, tall and blond, and his height made him stand out in the crowd, but she could have recognized him anyway from the bewildered expression on his face.

"I am Jess Stanton," she said as he drew closer. "I have identification."

He shook his head. "No, no. That's all right. I believe you. It's just that Thorpe—" He shook his head. "You just won't do. You'd better get a flight back."

Jess fought the sinking feeling in the pit of her stomach. "Mr. Harrington, I came here in good faith to accept an assignment. You can't just dismiss me like this! Mr. Thorpe admired my work. That's why he sent for me."

Harrington shook his head again. "I know all that. But it doesn't matter. I know Thorpe. He wouldn't think of taking a woman into the jungle."

"But I'm not a woman! That is, I'm a photographer. And a good one, too. This isn't fair."

Harrington smiled ruefully. "Thorpe doesn't worry about things like fairness. Thorpe, Phillips, and Thorpe is one of the biggest and richest law firms in the city. Thorpe's used to getting things his own way."

"Well, this time he'll have to give a little. I accepted this assignment in good faith and I intend to fulfill it."

"But you can't." Harrington was obviously embarrassed. "Thorpe will just send you packing."

"Then let him do his own dirty work," said Jess firmly. "I at least have the right to see him. I haven't traveled halfway around the world just to be sent away without that much satisfaction."

Harrington looked even more embarrassed. "For your own good I wish you'd take my advice and go now. Thorpe has no use for women in the jungle. He simply won't allow it."

Jess drew herself up to her full five feet four inches.

"Mr. Harrington, I appreciate your position. I really do. But if you don't get me through customs and take me to see this arrogant boss of yours, I am going to raise such a terrible stink that all of the city will know about it before I'm through. How will your Mr. Thorpe like that?"

Harrington managed a small smile. "There's very little in the way of scandal that hasn't already been spread about Thorpe. His adventures with various women—" He stopped suddenly, as though aware he had said too much.

"Well, I certainly can't leave you here. And since you won't take a flight home, I guess I'll have to take you out to the house."

"Thank you," said Jess, aware that her stomach was tying itself in knots. This Harrington didn't know it, but she actually had no recourse but to stay in Singapore. The ticket had been one way and outfitting herself had used up all her remaining cash. She could not *afford* a ticket home.

If she had not already known something of Thorpe's power, she might have deduced it quite readily in the minutes that followed. At a word from Harrington she was ushered through customs with what could only be termed deference and out to a waiting car. It was all done so quickly that she could scarcely believe it—and without even a cursory look into her bags.

As the driver pulled away from the airport, she leaned eagerly toward the window. Harrington smiled. "Singapore is an exciting city. Perhaps you should spend a few days sightseeing before going back to the States."

Jess did not reply. She was too busy trying to take in everything as the car proceeded down the road and through the city toward Mt. Faber. There was so much that it was hard to keep a distinct picture of anything.

But the things that made the strongest impression on her overburdened senses were the store signs—long, narrow banners of cloth, they hung above each store, their strange unreadable symbols huge against bright backgrounds.

The streets were crowded with people and Jess saw more women in cheongsams and saris and Malay women in sarongs. The men did not catch her eye as often as the women, perhaps because so many of them wore traditional Western garb, though here and there she saw men in their old style clothes. She pointed out a dark, bearded man in a turban to Harrington.

"That's a Sikh," he said. "Fierce warriors. Their religion forbids the cutting of their hair. The men wear it all curled up inside their turbans."

Jess smiled. "You know a lot. Have you been in Singapore long, Mr. Harrington?"

"Long enough," he replied. "My father and Derek's were friends. He and I grew up together."

"Oh." Jess was reluctant to learn any more about Mr. Derek Thorpe. She was already nursing quite a bit of anger against him. Anything that made him more a human and less a tyrant would only hamper her in her efforts to defend herself. If she had judged him correctly, Derek Thorpe could only be swayed by an aggressive attack. She had met such men before and their resistance was best overcome by meeting anger with anger. No feminine tears, no hint of surrender, and, most of all, no recognition of any blame. If Derek Thorpe had believed her a man and mistakenly made her an offer based on that assumption, that was *his* problem. She did not intend to make it hers. She wanted this assignment very badly and she intended to fight for it.

The car moved out of the city and up toward Mt.

Faber. Jess, trying to think of ways to meet Thorpe's attack, was only vaguely aware of the rich, well-kept homes set in lush grounds that they passed.

She was still not prepared as the driver pulled off the road into a private drive. The house was hidden from the road by vegetation and a winding drive and as they rounded a corner and came full upon it, Jess gasped. It was a lovely house of a great sprawling design that seemed to blend right into the earth itself.

"What unusual wood," she murmured.

"It's built of teak. Derek designed it himself. Imported the teak from Burma."

"I see."

The car pulled up to the big front door, flanked by great bushes of jasmine. Their heavy fragrance filled the air as she stepped out.

Harrington frowned. "I still think this is a mistake."

Jess managed a smile. "Are you trying to scare me, Mr. Harrington?"

"The name is Dick," he said. "And I am trying to warn you—nothing more." His face crinkled into a warm smile. "You're just a little bit of a thing. And Derek—well, Derek is Derek." He shrugged. "You haven't the slightest chance of changing his mind."

Jess shrugged. "Nevertheless, I intend to try. A contract is a contract, Mr.—Dick. Even Derek Thorpe should know that."

Harrington said no more and giving the driver orders to wait, he escorted her to the door. In moments it was opened by a tiny, wizened Chinese woman wearing a blue blouse and black trousers. Even beside Jess this woman seemed small.

"Good day, Ah Cheng," said Harrington.

"Good day, Mr. Harrington. Master Derek expect you." Her black eyes came to rest on Jess. "But this—"

"This is the photographer."

"Photographer?" It was obvious from the old woman's expression that she too had expected a man.

"She is going to meet Mr. Thorpe," said Harrington and he and Ah Cheng exchanged glances.

Jess, feeling her knees begin to tremble, said staunchly, "Come, don't tell me any more horror stories. Just lead me to him."

"As you wish," said Harrington soberly and, taking her elbow, he guided her down a spacious hall to a closed door. "This is his office. I will let you settle matters with him alone. You might fare better that way." And before she could answer he had moved away.

Jess took a deep breath. There was no use in putting off the inevitable. After all, Derek Thorpe was only a man. She raised her hand and knocked briskly.

"Come in." The voice was startling in its depth and vibrance.

Jess pushed open the door and entered. She tried to do it boldly and confidently. Whatever effect she had achieved was lost, however, since the man behind the great desk was engrossed with some papers.

And then he looked up. Jess felt her heart rise up in her throat. He was a man of almost forty. He wore a tropical-weight off-white suit, obviously expertly tailored, and a sky blue silk shirt open at the neck. The man himself was dark, bronzed by the sun and with a mass of curly dark hair touched with gray and the sort of ruggedly handsome face that many women find irresistible. But his eyes were his most outstanding feature. They were the gray of concrete—and just as cold and hard.

He scrutinized her and then asked harshly, "Who the devil are you and what are you doing in my house?"

Jess felt her mouth go suddenly dry. No wonder

Harrington had left her alone. This man fairly oozed power.

"My name is Jess Stanton," she said crisply.

The cold gray eyes looked her over again and she was uncomfortably aware of her rumpled appearance. "Impossible. Jess Stanton is the photographer I hired for a trip into the Borneo jungle."

Jess felt her anger rising. "I *am* Jess Stanton," she repeated. "Would you like to see my passport?"

Thorpe shook his head. "That won't be necessary. You won't do."

Jess drew nearer to the desk. "Mr. Thorpe. You gave me this assignment on the strength of my work. May I remind you that that work has not changed?"

"You may remind me of anything you like," he said curtly. "But it'll do you no good. You are still a female. And there's no place in the jungle for a female." He dropped his eyes to the desk and picked up one of a pile of papers.

Now Jess was really angry. "Mr. Thorpe! I have spent a great deal of time getting here. I think you might have the courtesy to give me your full attention for a few moments."

The dark head came up again and something very like amusement flickered in his eyes. "Very well, Miss Stanton. You have my complete attention. However, I do not see that it will do you any good. It cannot change the fact that you are female. In fact," his eyes slid down her body, "it only serves to strengthen that impression."

Jess felt the color rushing to her cheeks but she refused to be deterred from her purpose. "I came to Singapore on an assignment. In good faith. And I expect to carry out that assignment."

Thorpe pushed back his chair and rose. He was not as tall as Harrington, but he still towered over her. And he moved with the grace of a great cat—a predator, Jess thought sharply as he came to a stop in front of her.

"Miss Stanton, you are not listening to me." He ran a strong brown hand through his dark curls. "This is a trip into the jungle interior, into the rain forest. It is not a Sunday School picnic we are discussing. The jungle is inhabited by many unfriendly creatures—crocodiles, snakes of all kinds, annoying insects, leeches."

He watched her closely. "Have you ever been bitten by leeches? Or attacked by a crocodile?"

Jess, who found the man's nearness disturbing, raised her eyes to his. "No to both your questions. But I have been attacked by a bobcat and rattlers. I have photographed bobcats, bears, rattlers, coyotes, and other wildlife in their natural habitats. And I assure you, I can handle anything you can."

For a moment longer Thorpe glared at her and then he burst into laughter—a deep, vibrant sound that Jess, in spite of her anger, found entrancing.

"I do not see anything particularly funny about my career," she said stiffly, determined not to yield to her sudden feeling of liking for this man.

"We have a Malay proverb that describes you accurately," he said with a smile. *"Anak kuching menjadi harimau."*

There was a moment's silence. "And what does that mean?" asked Jess.

"It means," he said with that disarming smile, "that the kitten is trying to become a tiger."

Jess stifled the urge to smile. If she were not careful, this man would charm her back on a plane to the States before she knew it.

"Mr. Thorpe," she began again.

"My name is Derek, Jess."

The sound of her name on his lips was like a caress

and Jess was swept by a sudden wave of sharp longing—for what she didn't even know.

"All right, Derek." She was careful to keep her voice crisp and businesslike. "You and I have an agreement. The letter with the ticket constitutes a contract. I am here to do my part."

"My dear Jess." The irony in his voice was heavy and this time the sound of her name made her wince. "I don't know how many others you have tricked into giving you assignments—"

"Tricked! That's not true. You saw my work. It's no trick."

Her chest was heaving now and she fought to control her anger.

"But it's signed Jess Stanton," he said smoothly.

"Of course it is. That's my name."

"Jess or Jessica?" he asked.

"I've been called Jess since I was two-years-old," she flared. "And I can photograph anything a man can. What are we going after anyway?"

"We *were* going to look for blooming Rafflesia and for a rare kind of nepenthe—pitcher plant. But you have ruined that."

She thought that perhaps he was baiting her, but she was far too angry to care. "It is you who have ruined everything," she said, aware that the tears were dangerously close and made even angrier by that awareness. "It was stupid of you not to specify if you had to have a man."

"I never considered that a female would do the work I saw in *National Wildlife*. It simply didn't cross my mind."

"And it didn't occur to me," retorted Jess sharply, "that a male would be so stupid as to insist that the sex of a photographer would show in his or her work."

She stood glaring at him. She knew she was behaving badly, but she really did not care. She was dirty and tired, jet lag was creeping up on her, and her chance at the big time was rapidly going down the drain. It seemed doubtful that anyone could convince this despot of anything, but she continued to try. "I am going to stay right here and do my job. And if you don't let me, I'm going to raise the biggest stink Singapore has ever seen."

He stared at her for a moment and then he laughed again. "Easy, kitten, sheathe your claws for a minute and let me think."

He stood silently lost in contemplation while Jess tried to calm herself. Her blood pressure must have skyrocketed, she thought. Working with this man would be more nerve-wracking than shooting rattlers. But exciting, too, said some perverse part of herself.

Finally Thorpe turned to her. "Well, Jess, you haven't convinced me. Not really. But the Rafflesia only blooms in July and to find another photographer at this late date would be impossible. So I guess we'll go ahead. But just remember this." He looked at her sternly. "You asked for this. So don't blame me for anything that happens."

"I certainly won't," she said crisply. "That would be very unbusinesslike."

Thorpe chuckled at this and for some insane reason Jess found herself asking, "Do you never take Mrs. Thorpe into the jungle?"

His eyes regarded her carefully. "There is no Mrs. Thorpe," he said finally. "And that is just an example of what I mean. A man would ask me outright if I had a wife. But not a woman. Oh no! She has to take the devious way around."

"Mr. Thorpe, I—"

"You must call me Derek, Jess," he said again in that

tone that was a caress. "And don't be upset because I see through your little machinations. I have had a great deal of experience with women." He gave her a cynical smile. "Though admittedly of a somewhat different kind."

There was a look in his eyes that gave Jess a strange feeling in the pit of her stomach, but she chose to ignore it.

"Since we have come to an agreement," she said in an even tone, "I should like to be shown to my room."

"The trip has left you exhausted," he said.

Something in his tone warned her and Jess smiled. He would not trap her that easily. "Indeed not," she replied. "But it has left me rather dirty. I should appreciate a chance to shower and change."

"Of course. Ah Cheng will show you to your room. If I know her, she will put you in a room somewhat more suitable than the one I had ordered."

Jess did not reply to this. She would never admit it to this arrogant man, but she *was* tired and after a nice bath she intended to take a little nap.

Almost as though he could read her mind, he smiled and said, "I should lie down for a while before dinner if I were you. That was a long trip. And jet lag can be pernicious."

Because she did not know how to answer this she merely nodded. She was finding the kind and charming Derek Thorpe almost more difficult to deal with than the angry arrogant one.

He turned away, giving her a view of his broad shoulders. Derek Thorpe, thought Jess as he slid behind his desk and buzzed for the servant, was going to be quite a man to work for.

"We'll discuss the other things, equipment, etc., later. For now you need a chance to settle in and rest. We have plenty of time."

There was a speculative look in his eyes that did more strange things to her stomach and she turned and pretended to study the view out the window until she heard the door open.

"Ah Cheng, this is our guest, Miss Stanton. She will be staying with us for some time."

Jess met the old woman's black eyes. Did she detect amusement there? It was impossible to tell.

Ah Cheng's expression was inscrutable as she replied, "Yes, sir. I have nice room for her."

"I thought you would," replied Thorpe with an enigmatic smile at Jess.

She remembered that smile a few minutes later as she stood in a daintily decorated bedroom that was obviously designed for a female occupant. The Chinese servant said, "I leave Miss now. Dinner at seven."

"Thank you."

The old woman smiled. "Master Derek, he is strong man. But he is not bad. Only strong."

Jess, wondering what had brought this on, could only reply, "He is very—unusual."

Ah Cheng's head bobbed in agreement. "Very unusual, Master Derek. And very good."

Jess would certainly have questioned this, but the servant stepped silently through the doorway. "We talk other time. You rest." Then she was gone.

Jess found all her cases lined up against the wall, but when she went to open one that held clothes, she found it empty. Pulling open a drawer in the antique white dresser, she found, incredibly, that all her clothes had been put away. How could Ah Cheng have known that she would be staying? She was too tired to puzzle that one out and she slipped quickly out of her clothes and into the bath that adjoined the room.

The sight made her stop and draw in her breath. The room was done in shades of peach and brown and gave such an impression of luxury that it startled her. The tub, big enough to walk into, was sunk into the floor and made of glazed peach-colored tile. It was surrounded on two sides by mirrors.

Jess kept her eyes averted from the reflection of herself that showed there. Someone had already drawn the water and she slipped into the bubble-filled tub with a feeling of unrealness. This was obviously the room in which Derek Thorpe housed his various 'female' guests, housed them in a luxury that she could not even have imagined.

As she lay back in the relaxing water, Jess tried to decide on a course of action. This assignment was vitally important to her career. It was her chance to get a spread in a really big magazine. And, of course, the fee that Thorpe had promised her would give her the time to do some interesting free-lance stuff later. Yes, this was her big chance and she didn't want to muff it. She would have to figure out what made Derek Thorpe tick. Besides women.

Idly she made motions in the bubbles. Yes, Derek Thorpe was obviously a man who liked the ladies. Well, she straightened with an abrupt motion that set up waves in the tub, if Mr. Derek Thorpe thought he was going to play the usual male/female games with his photographer, he had another think coming. This was going to be a business deal. Strictly business and nothing else.

She stayed in the water for some time, feeling a curious lethargy creep over her. Finally she forced herself to get up and dry. She would just have a little sleep before dinner. She reached for a towel that had nap an inch thick. It was like drying her body on velvet, she thought vaguely as she made her way back to the bedroom.

The bed looked most inviting. Ah Cheng had removed the pale peach spread and the sheets of the same hue had been turned down invitingly. She was far too tired to search for a nightgown, thought Jess as she slid between the sheets. They were incredibly smooth and soft against her naked skin. Silk! she thought with a sense of shock—real silk. She stretched and sighed. So this was how they lived—the very rich.

She closed her eyes, but the lethargy that had almost overcome her in the water seemed to desert her now. The silk seemed almost alive against her skin and her imagination began to consider what might have occurred in this room, in this very bed. The thought did nothing to relax her.

Why had Derek Thorpe had her put in this room, this room which was so obviously designed for another kind of woman? It was true that Thorpe had not said anything about a particular room to Ah Cheng, but he had seemed to know what the woman would do. And he had been amused by the whole idea.

Jess turned restlessly in the bed. She had never taken much interest in men as romantic objects. She had lost both her parents when she was eighteen and the three years since then she had been scrabbling to get a foothold in her profession. It wasn't easy to break into any field, especially the one Jess had chosen. Thorpe had been right in assuming that most wilderness photographers were men. But not all.

Jess flopped onto her other side. Of course, she had run into men who had been eager to give her a boost up the ladder to success. And who inevitably expected something from her in return.

She knew she was old-fashioned in some respects and perhaps coming from the Montana hills had made her too proud. But she simply could not see selling herself for some man's help. She would make it on her own, she told herself stubbornly, on the strength of her work—or not at all.

She flopped over again. There had been a couple of times—after all, she was human—when she had been attracted to a young man. But those inevitably ended in disaster when the man discovered that she did not intend to give up her career after marriage. And so in the last year or two she had had few dates and she had not really cared.

But there was something about Derek Thorpe that intrigued her. Something more than the contrast of his white suit against bronze skin, or the way his dark, curly chest hair spilled out the neck of his shirt, or the ruggedly handsome face with its stubborn chin and cold gray eyes. There was an aura of power about him, but it was even more than that. It was, thought the now wide-awake Jess, an aura of virile masculinity, of stark, raw maleness. Derek Thorpe gave off very powerful male vibrations—and, unfortunately, he knew it.

Suddenly Jess threw back the sheet and jumped to her feet. There was no chance of her sleeping now. She felt a strange restlessness. She must *do* something.

Through the screened French doors that opened onto the veranda she saw an array of flowers. That was it; she would dress and go for a walk in the garden.

She turned toward the closet, fully intending to reach for another pant suit, but somehow her hand came out with a pale green sundress. It was a simple dress that she had included at the last minute as something suitable for shopping in hot weather.

She slipped into her underpants and bra and pulled the dress over her head, slid into a pair of sandals, and ran a comb through her hair.

There. She must get out of this room for a while. Though moments ago she had been quite cool and she could certainly turn the air conditioning up, she felt as though she could not breath.

She pushed open the French doors and stepped out onto a wide teak veranda. A lawn chair seemed to beckon invitingly, but it was too close to that room. Looking around her, she saw that the veranda seemed to extend around three sides of the house, which from this angle seemed even larger. The house itself was ingeniously built into the side of the mountain and the garden spread out around it in terraces.

The veranda had no rail and it was a simple matter to step from it down into the garden. Flowers grew everywhere, riotous clouds of pink, blue, yellow, white, orange, purple, and red surrounded her. Some flowers Jess could recognize: magnolias and jasmine, hibiscus and frangipani. Others she had never seen before. She breathed deeply of their fragrance.

The garden was shaded by many small trees, some of which were also in bloom. And tall hedges, crowned with blossoms, separated various terraces from each other and made little private places.

Like a child Jess wandered from flower to flower, examining each different blossom, thinking how gloriously the colors would film, drinking in the fragrance.

The grass, a lush deep green, was littered by fallen magnolia blossoms. Jess found a little stone bench in the shade and sank down on it. Again that curious lethargy was stealing over her. She felt as though she could sit for hours in the sweet coolness and not think at all.

She had no idea how long she had sat there, feeling at peace with herself and the world, quietly enjoying the blossoms and the fragrance that surrounded her, when it suddenly occurred to her to wonder about the time. A look at her watch sent her to her feet. Oh dear, it was after seven and Ah Cheng had said dinner was served at seven. She had already antagonized the powerful Mr. Thorpe enough; it was certainly not smart—or even in good taste—to be late for dinner. She flushed now at the memory of the foolish way she had threatened him. Why, Derek Thorpe was so powerful. He could crush her like the smallest of gnats and not even feel her sting.

Half in panic, she gazed around her. Which way was the house? Fortunately, as she turned she discovered that the roof of the house was directly behind her. She began to hurry in that direction. Now the many turnings and little private spots surrounded by hedges no longer seemed beautiful. Whoever had designed the gardens had obviously not given much thought to the problems of a stranger who was late for dinner.

The pleasant coolness of the evening seemed to vanish and Jess felt the perspiration beading her forehead. She was behaving foolishly, and she knew it. Derek Thorpe was certainly not going to change his mind simply because she was late to dinner. And it was absolutely ridiculous to feel like a bad little girl.

Still, she quickened her steps and so she was almost running as she rounded a corner of hedge and ran headlong into a male chest. In the split second before she came crashing to a halt, Jess recognized the blue shirt. Then the breath was knocked from her and she really needed the strong arms that steadied her.

There was a long moment of silence and Jess was acutely conscious of the beating of his heart beneath her ear and the feel of the crisp curling chest hair that had escaped at the open throat of his shirt and lay against her cheek.

Then Thorpe spoke. "So there you are, kitten. What's chasing you?"

There was a sort of sardonic humor in his tone and Jess looked up to meet his eyes. "Nothing's chasing me," she managed to say. "I just realized that I was late for dinner."

Thorpe chuckled and Jess thought again how very pleasant the sound was. "You must be starving to be in such a hurry."

His arms did not release her and Jess was so conscious of his nearness that she found it difficult to gather her wits. "I—I did not want to be late."

"What a considerate guest you are."

He was laughing at her and she knew it. Jess knew, too, that she should move out of those arms, away from the wide chest clad in blue silk. But he had not lowered his arms and, besides that, she was uneasily aware that she did not want to move.

"How do you like my house?" he asked.

"I have never been in such a place before," she said honestly. "I was born and raised on a ranch in Montana. It's not very luxurious there."

"And how did you find your room?" His eyes were full of amusement and she was irritably aware that she flushed.

Perhaps that was what prompted her to reply, "It seems a little overdone."

His eyes narrowed and then his lips curved into a devilish grin. "My kitten believes in honesty, I see."

Jess heard the 'my' and knew she should correct him. She was not his and she was not a kitten. But somehow she knew if she said anything to that effect he would probably only laugh. It seemed unlikely that any woman had rejected Derek Thorpe for some time and the longer she stood in the circle of his arms the less sure she was of her own resolve.

"We will be late for dinner," she said, but Thorpe did not seem to hear her. He was gazing into her eyes in a way she found most disconcerting.

"If you do not like the room," he said gravely. "I will have it redone."

Jess looked at him sharply, but he seemed to be completely serious. "Don't be ridiculous," she said. "It is only that I'm not that kind of woman—that is—I'm not at home in that sort of room." She felt the red flooding her cheeks again. It was none of her business what Derek Thorpe did with his private life.

"I see. You disapprove of such frivolity."

He was scrutinizing her carefully and she felt that she had already said the wrong thing. "I—I'm used to simple things."

He nodded. "But just because you are accustomed to living in the wilderness, that doesn't mean that you can't enjoy some sensuous pleasures. After all, you are a female."

Jess, whose heart was pounding from such close contact with this most virile of men, thought bitterly that she needed no reminder of that. Certainly not at this moment.

"Just relax, kitten. Relax and enjoy."

She knew there was something wrong with this reasoning, but she could not gather her wits to refute it. And then, with an ease that spoke of a great deal of practice, Derek Thorpe bent his head and kissed her. It was a strange kiss—more powerful than any Jess had ever known. By turns tender, persuasive, and passionate, it seemed to rob her of her will. She fought to keep from responding to it, but it was a losing battle. And when finally he released her, she found that her arms had crept up to circle his neck, her heart was pounding in her throat, and the strength seemed to have gone out of her legs.

"There," he said with a lazy smile. "See? You *are* female."

Jess stiffened, sudden anger coursing through her. Who did he think he was anyway? She was not going to be like the previous occupants of that room—not by a long shot.

She put all the acid she could into her voice as she replied, "I am sorry to disappoint you, Mr. Thorpe. But I was hired as a photographer. And those are the *only* duties I intend to perform."

For a long moment he remained silent and then his eyes narrowed and his arms fell away from her. "Of course, Miss Stanton," he replied formally. "Those were the only duties I expected from you." His eyes grew colder. "I generally choose partners who are warm, feminine women."

She felt as though he had slapped her, but she could not in good conscience blame him. Certainly she had given far too much importance to what was probably merely a friendly kiss. But, she told herself, with her body behaving so strangely and her head awhirl from his nearness how could she be expected to behave sensibly?

"Now that we clearly understand each other, perhaps we should go in to dinner. My chef is excellent but he can only keep a dinner edible for so long."

"Yes, of course," replied Jess, hoping that her tone sounded normal.

As she followed Derek Thorpe back to the house she wondered if she had made a mistake. How could she expect to do good work when the man's mere presence sent her senses tumbling about like so many fox cubs playing in springtime?

The trip back to the house was made in silence and Jess grew more and more embarrassed. She had really been unforgivably rude to the man and now she could hardly blame him for thinking poorly of her. It seemed rather obvious that most women considered a kiss from

Derek Thorpe a pleasure. And well they should, she caught herself thinking. For certainly the man was an expert at it.

Thorpe turned as they reached the house. "The veranda goes around three sides of the house. If we follow it, we will reach the dining room quicker."

Jess could only nod. She was very hot and she had completely lost her appetite, but she did not dare say so. She did not want to chance offending him further.

"There will be others for dinner," Thorpe said.

Involuntarily Jess glanced down at her simple dress.

"It doesn't matter," he said with a smile that did nothing to reassure her. "After all, you don't care about such frivolities anyway."

Jess fought a sudden urge to scream and was surprised at the violence of her reaction. Never had she met another human being who was so completely maddening. She forced herself to remain calm. "Who are the others?" she asked.

"Harrington, of course. He'll be going to Sarawak and Sabah with us. And Haviland will be here."

"Haviland?" Jess was bewildered. Was this other guest male or female?

"Haviland Phillips, daughter of my retired partner. She dines here often."

"Oh." Jess said nothing more, but she felt a shiver of distaste. Haviland seemed like a very cold name. And what exactly was Miss Phillips' connection to Derek Thorpe? If she was the daughter of the retired Mr. Phillips, she must have known Thorpe for quite a long time. Jess prepared herself for an uncomfortable evening. Quite probably if Miss Phillips had some interest in Thorpe she would not like the idea of him going off into the jungle with another woman.

Jess straightened her shoulders. This job had certainly turned out to be more than she had bargained for.

But she intended to stick it out no matter how uncomfortable Derek Thorpe tried to make— She almost stopped in mid-stride. Had Thorpe had her put in that room, and kissed her as he had, deliberately? Hoping that she would pack up and leave?

Jess's lips tightened into a thin line. If that was his purpose, then he would fail in it. Miserably.

They entered the dining room through a huge pair of sliding French doors. Jess saw that the room was paneled in teak and that in its center sat a great teakwood table surrounded by chairs. She shifted her attention to the room's occupants. Harrington smiled and she felt a sense of comfort. At least she had one friend in the room. And then Thorpe was guiding her around the table to where another woman stood. And what a woman, Jess thought bitterly. Her light blond hair was piled high on top of her head. She wore a dress of deep green silk that even to Jess's untutored eyes looked very expensive. It sported a deep V-neck, one that Jess knew with terrible certainty she herself could never wear in public. The dress clung to Miss Phillips in a way that left very little to the imagination. Around her neck and in her ears hung what must be real diamonds. Jess swallowed the lump in her throat. She was far out of her league here. There was no way she could compete with a woman like this.

And then, realizing what she was thinking, she pulled herself up short. She had no intentions of competing with Haviland Phillips or any other woman. Hadn't she just informed her employer—and rather sharply too— that their relationship was to be strictly business?

Derek Thorpe, his hand on her elbow, guided her forward. "This is the photographer for our trip. Jess Stanton, Haviland Phillips."

Jess moved her eyes to the woman's face. It was a

beautiful face, molded in classic lines. Like that of a marble statue. And just as cold. A pair of chill green eyes surveyed Jess condescendingly. "A *woman* photographer?"

Derek Thorpe laughed and his hand tightened on Jess's elbow in a way that did something strange to her stomach. "That was precisely what *I* said, wasn't it Jess?"

He turned to her with such a jovial smile that she could only nod. What had happened to transform the coldly formal man of moments earlier into this genial charmer?

"But," he continued. "Jess insists that she can handle the jungle."

"Ugh!" Miss Phillips' classic nose wrinkled in distaste. "The jungle is no place for a woman."

"My sentiments precisely," agreed Thorpe. "But Jess feels otherwise. She has her career to think of."

The words were right; they made quite good sense. But something was wrong with his tone. Jess raised her eyes to his and knew immediately that she was right. Cynical amusement was shining there.

"Sometimes," she replied stiffly, "women consider their careers as important as men do."

Something flickered in his eyes and was gone. "Really?"

"Really."

Dick Harrington moved closer. "It's good to see you again, Miss Stanton," he said with a friendly grin, running one hand through his straight blond hair.

"Please call me Jess," she replied, returning his smile. "It looks like I'm going to see something of Malaysia after all."

"It does indeed." Harrington continued to smile. "And so you must call me Dick."

"Derek, can't we eat now?" Miss Phillips asked petulantly. "The Garden Club luncheon today was atrocious. Not fit for human consumption."

"Of course Haviland, my dear." Thorpe offered her his arm.

As the other woman took it, Jess bit back a sigh. It seemed doubtful to her that Haviland Phillips' pale complexion or long laquered nails had ever come close to a garden—at least in the daylight. In her mind she recalled the little nooks and crannies of the garden outside. Undoubtedly Haviland Phillips had been in them *often*.

As she settled in the chair that Harrington pulled out for her, she wondered what it was like to wear real silk and diamonds. To never do any work. To belong to Derek Thorpe, said a wild voice in her head.

But that was *not* what she wanted, she told herself sharply. And if Haviland Phillips was his idea of a warm feminine woman—well, the two of them certainly deserved each other!

# Chapter 2

When Jess opened her eyes the next morning, it took her a few moments to realize where she was. Then the feel of the silk sheets against her bare arms wakened her more completely; the memory of the previous day came pouring back. She sighed and rolled over. It hardly seemed possible that a person could be as politely nasty as Haviland Phillips had been. But certainly last night had proved it.

Jess frowned. She had always felt that she could hold her own with anyone, social class notwithstanding. Just because she had been born and raised on a ranch didn't mean she was ignorant. And Montana people were proud of themselves.

But last night she had felt pretty low. The price of gold or the demand for diamonds were not everyday affairs for her. She sighed. If only she hadn't been so confused and tired, *she* might have talked about the lastest color film or the newest thing in light meters. But, of course, she would have had to talk to herself since neither Thorpe nor Harrington were familiar with such things. No, she supposed it was better that she had kept silent. At least no one had laughed at her ignorance and Dick Harrington had been warmly friendly.

She turned onto her other side. It was too bad that Thorpe couldn't be friendly. She was still puzzling over her reactions to that man. Certainly in her twenty-one years she had known men, even been attracted to some of them. But never had she known a man like Derek Thorpe.

Perhaps it was his money that made him arrogant, so sure of his power. But somehow Jess felt that even if one day he were to lose everything, Derek Thorpe would still go merrily on his way, believing that the world was his own personal toy.

She threw back the covers. She might as well get up. There was no point in lying there reviewing the fiasco of dinner. Jess shook her head. She simply could not see how any man could regard Haviland Phillips as a warm feminine person. It was fairly obvious that she visited the beauty shop periodically. And she looked untouchable.

But Jess, recalling the strange feelings that Derek Thorpe raised in her, reconsidered this. Quite probably Thorpe could touch any woman he pleased.

She swung her feet to the floor and thought again how incongruous her simple cotton pajamas looked against the silk sheets. She had been entirely right about one thing. She was definitely not comfortable in this room.

She rose and stretched, then wandered over to the French doors. The sun was shining and the garden looked beautiful, but she knew from the guidebook that at this time of day it would be very hot and humid. Besides, she had work to do. There were supplies to be checked and lists to be gone over. After all, she was a working photographer, not a lady of leisure.

As she ran water into the tub Jess tried to analyze her attitude toward Haviland Phillips. She disliked the other woman and she was not entirely sure why. Any other time she would probably not have given any thought to Miss Phillips' obvious attempts to put her down. Ordinarily she would have laughed at such a woman. But she did not think it was funny this time. Not at all.

The question was why. Why had she let the rich and nasty Haviland get to her?

As she lay back in the scented water, Jess asked herself if she would trade places with Haviland Phillips. The answer was an emphatic no. Not even for the chance to belong to Derek Thorpe would she want to—

A startled exclamation burst from her lips. That was the crux of the matter. Haviland Phillips belonged to Derek Thorpe. She had the right to call him, to touch him, to be completely woman with him.

Jess grabbed a washcloth and began to scrub herself vigorously. She was being ridiculous. She had no interest in Derek Thorpe. She must keep to that thought. If they were going into the jungle together, it was sheer insanity to think otherwise. Besides, if and when she decided to love a man, she did not intend to share him with half the female population of Singapore!

She pulled the plug and got to her feet. Enough of this insanity. There was work to be done and she intended to do it.

Back in the bedroom she opened the closet door. Her eyes moved down the clothes hanging there. There were very few dresses—nothing that came anywhere near that green creation of Haviland Phillips. Mostly Jess wore simple clothes—slacks and blouses, and, for work in the wilderness, tough khakis. With a grimace she reached for a pair of green slacks and a cool white blouse.

It was the work of the moment to slip into this outfit and Jess turned to the mirror and ran a brush through her hair. It shone in the sunshine as it clustered in little curls. She shook her head; it certainly did not match Miss Phillips' stylized elegance.

She ran a lipstick lightly over her lips and turned to

go look for breakfast. Her stomach, which was used to regular early breakfasts, was complaining and no amount of time spent before her mirror would give her that look of glazed elegance that characterized Haviland Phillips.

Jess stepped out into the hall. Now, which way to the kitchen? She decided to start first in the dining room and made her way in that direction. She realized suddenly that her knees were wobbly and knew that it was because she might run into Derek Thorpe.

But the hall was silent and empty and she reached the dining room without seeing anyone. She was about to open the door through which the servants had brought the dinner, when it opened to disclose a Chinese man. He was bent over and he moved slowly. "Miss up early. You wanting breakfast?"

Jess nodded.

"You sit here. Loh Ah Cheng will bring."

Jess looked at the great table. "Couldn't I eat in the kitchen? Would Loh Ah Cheng mind?"

"She not mind," said the little man. "You follow me."

Soon Jess was happily seated at a little table in the spotless kitchen. "You want American breakfast—bacon, eggs, toast?" asked the Chinese woman.

"That sounds great Loh Ah Cheng."

"You call me Ah Cheng. That my what-you-call 'first' name. Loh my last name. In China last name come first. Right away know what family you belong."

"Thank you Ah Cheng. Will you call me Jess?"

The old woman shook her head. "Not right. Call you Miss. Call Mr. Thorpe, Master Derek. I know since he was baby. I nurse."

It was hard for Jess to think of the hardhitting, powerful Thorpe as a tiny helpless baby. She looked at Ah Cheng with curiosity. "Did he cry a lot?"

The old servant shook her head. "Master Derek good baby. Not cry." Her face crinkled into a smile. "Little boy sometimes bad. But always keep going till he get what he want."

So, thought Jess, even as a little boy Derek Thorpe had been arrogant. "And his parents?" she asked as Ah Cheng separated slices of bacon.

"Very good people. We work for them long time. When we first come Singapore, we very young. Just married." She gestured to the little man. "His mother send us, earn money send home. We come to Singapore, Chinatown, Upper Nankin Street. We get our own place. Very small." Ah Cheng made a small square with her hands. "Nine paces each way. No window to outside. Go through neighbors to go out."

"Wasn't that hard?"

Ah Cheng nodded. "Then one day," she continued, "girls in coolie-fang (place where many working girls live together), tell about Mrs. Thorpe. Beautiful lady need nurse for baby. I have baby just gone to ancestors." She bowed her head briefly. "Still have milk. Master Derek become my baby. Mrs. Thorpe hire me for nurse. But I tell her I need Lim Giok Leng." She gazed at her husband fondly. "She make him gardener. We both very happy then. Have our own rooms, very nice. Much money to send home to China."

"And so you stayed on," said Jess.

Ah Cheng nodded. "When Mr. and Mrs. Thorpe killed in airplane crash, Master Derek say he need us. We stay forever."

The picture of Derek Thorpe admitting to a need was a surprising one to Jess, but she made no comment except to ask, "How old was he then? When he lost them?"

Ah Cheng considered. "I think just twenty. Just back from school in England. Very bad time for him."

Jess tried to think of Thorpe in these circumstances and could not. "How did he manage?"

"Mr. Phillips help him. Master Derek go away, learn to be lawyer. Already have much money. Learn to make much more."

Ah Cheng served up bacon, eggs, and toast with a flourish. "Good American breakfast. You like."

Jess, digging in with a will, found that she did indeed 'like.' "This is very good," she said between mouthfuls. "Very good."

Ah Cheng nodded in thanks for the praise and then frowned. "Not cook much now. Master Derek get this new chef. Funny Frenchman. Talk strange. Wear tall hat."

Ah Cheng puffed out her cheeks in such an imitation of pomposity that Jess broke into laughter. "Perhaps Mr. Thorpe wants to spare you that work."

The servant shook her head. "Not so. Master Derek always like what I cook. Till Miss Haviland come back from finishing school." The little housekeeper's black eyes gleamed. "That school spoil Miss Haviland. Not a person anymore. Just a stuffed doll, like buy in Change Alley."

Not knowing how to respond to this, Jess pushed back her empty plate. "That was the best meal I've had in ages. Thank you."

Ah Cheng bowed. "I thank you. I like talk. Most Master Derek visitors no talk. Only give orders."

Jess smiled. "I like talking to you. I'd like to hear more about China."

Ah Cheng smiled again. "I tell you. I like talk about old times. I tell you about my wedding."

"Good," said Jess. "I'd stay now but I have to check out my equipment."

Ah Cheng nodded. "Very good. Maybe we talk tomorrow. I make American breakfast again. Maybe pancakes? I tell you many things."

Jess laughed. "That sounds great, really great. I'll see you then. Thank you."

Ah Cheng bowed again. "I have happiness to do this."

Giok Leng nodded. "That right. She always complain. No one to cook for but me."

Jess thanked the old couple again and made her way back to her room. This was the first time she had ever been outside of the States and the story of the conditions in which Ah Cheng had begun her married life seemed appalling to her. Living in a cubicle nine feet by nine feet. She simply could not imagine such a thing. The problems of simple sanitation staggered her mind.

No wonder the old pair revered Thorpe as they did. His parents had saved them from a life of abject poverty. And, too, Ah Cheng had been a kind of foster mother to the baby. How painful it must have been to lose her own child. It was easy to see how she could have given the love her dead child could no longer use to the living child at her breast.

Jess began to open her cases and lay out equipment, but her mind was not on her task. It was busy creating pictures of a young Chinese woman smiling fondly at the baby in her arms.

Finally Jess had things in order and had double-checked her list of needed supplies. It would never do to run out of some vital thing like film when they were somewhere in the jungle. With a sigh she separated the darkroom equipment from the rest. Conditions in the jungle being what they were it would be impossible to set up an adequate darkroom there. This considerably complicated matters. Since she would have no way of knowing how her pictures were going to come out, she would of necessity be forced to take more than the usual number of shots—as a kind of insurance. Her imagination presented her with a vivid picture of Derek Thorpe's face if by some mischance the film should be spoiled. It was not a pretty picture and she shoved it from her mind. She had plenty of waterproof cases in which to carry the rolls that had been shot. The cases should protect against dampness, humidity, and bugs.

Restlessly Jess moved away from the bed. Thorpe had mentioned leeches in the jungle. The thought made her shiver. The most ferocious animals did not bother her like the insects and other forms of life that even the tightest-fitting clothes would not protect against.

She swung on her heel and began to pace back and forth. This was no time to chicken out. She had photographed mountain lions in their lairs, coyotes in their dens. Tracked bears into the wilderness and rattlers into the rocks. She did not intend to back down at the prospect of a few yucky leeches. Still, she did not find the idea particularly appealing.

So, they were going to get shots of the Rafflesia, Jess told herself. She had a very vague idea of reading about the plant in the literature she had gotten about Malaysia. But at that time it had no significance for her.

She shrugged and began to repack her equipment. What she would like to photograph was Ah Cheng's wrinkled face. There was so much character there. The thought rather surprised Jess as she had never considered doing portraits.

The shrill ringing of the phone caused her to jump, startled. She hurried across the room to pick it up. "Hello?"

"Jess, this is Thorpe." Over the phone his voice was even deeper and more vibrant. Jess felt a shiver go over here "We're having a meeting about the expedition at the office at twelve," he continued. "We'll lunch. Can you be ready with your lists?"

"Of course." She barely stopped herself from saying 'Mr. Thorpe,' but added no name to her statement. "I have it ready now."

"Good girl."

Jess felt herself stiffen. There was that condescending tone again! How irritating the man could be. She thought about calling him to task for it, but decided against it. He would probably only laugh and call her something even more degrading, like 'kitten.'

"I'll see you at twelve. So long."

"Wait! Mr. Thorpe! Where *is* the office?"

His voice conveyed his annoyance so clearly that she could almost see the expression on his face. "Relax. I'll send a car for you, of course. That's all. Goodbye."

"Goodbye."

Jess waited till she heard him hang up and then dropped the receiver back sharply. Of course he would send the car! Of course! And just how was she supposed to know that? A girl from the Montana hills whose major concern about any car was that its engine be reliable, had little experience with cars that came and went by themselves.

She supposed that if she had thought the matter through she might have remembered the car that had picked her and Harrington up at the airport. She saw now that it must have been Thorpe's car. But at the time she had been too busy to notice such things. Living amid such luxury was a difficult task, she thought with a grim smile. At least for her.

As she finished packing things away, she remembered the first little apartment she had had in Billings. It couldn't have been very big. But she had been very comfortable there after the ranch was sold. How odd that she should be more comfortable in poverty than in luxury, she told herself as she stacked the cases against the wall. But then it probably had to do with what one knew best. Derek Thorpe might not manage well in poverty. But then again, he might.

She finished the last case and looked at her watch. Already it was eleven. The morning seemed to have flown by. Perhaps she would take another bath and relax before she faced the high-handed Mr. Thorpe.

She turned toward the closet. What did one wear to a business conference with a man like Thorpe she wondered, wishing that by some miracle she could appear as faultlessly dressed as the uppity Haviland Phillips. Suddenly realizing the trend of her thoughts, Jess exclaimed in disgust. Wouldn't she look ridiculous? No one could wade through jungle streams and climb mountains while preserving the chic, fashionable look that seemed to be Haviland. Derek Thorpe would undoubtedly see her dirty, sweaty, and exhausted, as he would be himself.

As she opened the closet door her eyes lit on her one good dress, a creation of soft cream polyester. When she bought it, she had considered it an extravagance, even though it was on sale. And its deep boat neckline and long full sleeves were not her usual style. But it had been on sale and just once she had given in to the temptation to own something soft and feminine, something besides the khakis and boots that were her working clothes. For a moment her hand moved toward the dress and then she shook her head. No! If she showed up in Thorpe's office in that dress, he would laugh at her or at the very least look at her with scorn. Justifiably, too, for such clothes would certainly not be much of an advertisement for a hardworking jungle photographer.

She was getting silly, Jess told herself. She was usually quite levelheaded and not at all susceptible to the influences of men—no matter how deep their voices or virile their appearances. Derek Thorpe was just another man and this was just another assignment.

She chose a pair of worn khaki pants and a shirt of cream-colored cotton. She would look as worklike as possible for this meeting.

Laying her clothes on the bed, Jess went into the bathroom and began to run the tub full of water, absently sprinkling in bath salts from one of the assorted jars on the glass vanity. The sweet aroma of flowers filled the air as Jess turned her back on the mirrored walls and began to undress. She just could not get used to seeing herself like that. A full view of her whole body without clothes—from several angles yet—was very disconcerting to her.

She slid into the perfumed water with a sigh and tried to relax. She was getting addicted to this tub and its soothing properties. Never had she been so uptight about a job. And she had worked with many men, big brawny men, virile men, very attractive men. None of them had ever disturbed her thinking as Derek Thorpe did.

Idly she swished the water around her. What made a man like Derek Thorpe tick? How had he managed to become so cocksure? Of course, there was no answer to that question.

Finally she stepped out of the tub and reached for a towel. That was another thing that was difficult to get used to. Her towels disappeared as soon as she used them once, taken, she supposed, by some silent invisible maid, who also replenished the huge stack on the fancy stand. It was that same maid, she supposed, who had made her bed and straightened her room while she was having breakfast.

The whole idea made Jess slightly uncomfortable. She was not used to being waited on; it made her as uneasy as the sumptuous furnishings of these rooms. Well, she told herself with an ironic smile, when she made *her* million she would certainly not waste it on an extravagantly furnished home. That would be dumb anyway since she spent most of her time on assignment. However, thought Jess with another smile, she did like that big tub.

Usually when she came back from a long assignment in the wilderness, the tub was the first thing she headed for. That was the thing she most longed for when, tired and dirty, she fell asleep in her tent at night.

She hung the towel on a rack and went back into the bedroom. It was a matter of minutes to slip into her underwear, pull on the blouse and slacks. A comb through her unruly red curls and another touch of lipstick and Jess was ready. She did not bother with other makeup except on some particularly important date. And certainly this could not be classified as a date.

She paced the floor nervously for a few minutes and then exclaimed angrily again. She was behaving very foolishly. Back in Montana, growing up on the ranch, she had done all the things the boys did. Fished, and swam, and rode the ponies. Even killed rattlers when the need arose. For her there had never been a frilly white bedroom or fancy dresses.

But then, she hadn't wanted those things. What she had wanted, with the desperation that only the very young can feel, was a camera of her own. She could not remember when she had first become fascinated with recording the things she saw around her. She had a blurred memory of wanting to capture the look of her goldfish as it swam in water reflecting sunbeams. And she had a very distinct memory of the Christmas she was ten, the Christmas she got her first camera.

It hadn't been anything spectacular, just an ordinary

camera. But to her it had been the most wonderful present in the world.

Somewhere in the house a clock chimed and Jess glanced at her watch. Perhaps she should walk out to the living room and wait for the car. She would not want to keep the great Mr. Thorpe waiting. She sighed. Bitterness was not like her at all. But everything in her life seemed different now.

Some minutes later, feeling rather ridiculous, Jess was seated in the car, being driven toward the city. She had left the window between herself and the driver open. For some reason she felt less silly that way, less like a little girl pretending to be a grown-up lady.

"Where does this road go to in the other direction?" she asked the driver, a small smiling man with ivory skin.

"This road goes to the top of Mount Faber," he replied in such perfect English that Jess started.

"I am Eurasian," he said. "My father was British. My mother Japanese-Chinese. My father sent me to England to school."

"But you are a chauf—" Jess stopped. She had no right to pry.

He continued. "I write poetry—haikus." He shrugged. "For such work there is little market, no money to speak of. But I love to write. My father was a novelist, but he always had to work to provide for us. I took this job because it gave me enough to live on and send some home—and time, time to write."

"I see." What a curious collection of servants Derek Thorpe had. Who had ever heard of a chauffeur who wrote poetry!

"What road is this?" she asked.

"This is Nelson Road," he said. "Then we will take New Bridge Road across the Singapore River—the Singapura as it used to be called."

"Do you know why?" asked Jess. She was vaguely aware that one of her reasons for asking so many questions was to keep her mind occupied and off the coming meeting with Thorpe.

"The city's name comes from the Sanskrit, Singa Pura, which means lion city. Long ago before the advent of Islam, Indian influence was greatest here."

"For some reason I thought the word might be Malay."

The driver shook his head. "The Malays called the city Tumasik—Sea Town."

"Oh," Jess replied.

"Have you seen any of the city?" the driver asked.

"Only a glimpse on the way to the house," Jess admitted.

"I will take you through Chinatown. It is not really out of our way. The Chinese began to emigrate in 1819, the same year Sir Stamford Raffles landed here and established a British settlement. Visit a Chinese temple while you are here. They are not like Christian churches. No hushed whispering. People offer joss sticks and burn prayers inscribed on red paper. They do it noisily, joyfully."

"Why do they *burn* their prayers?" asked Jess.

"So that the ashes may float up to the gods and the prayers will be answered."

"Of course," cried Jess, thinking that there was a great deal of logic to the whole idea.

"My mother took me often to the temples when I was a boy. My very favorite is the Goddess of Mercy Temple, Kuan Yim Tong. I was intrigued by her eighteen hands."

"Eighteen hands? Why?"

"Each hand holds an object symbolic of her powers like a pot, a rope, a lotus flower, a bell, a sword, a magic mirror."

"What is she the goddess of?" inquired Jess.

"Of healing and destruction."

"I don't understand."

"Like many Asian dieties—and your own Christian god—Kuan Yim Tong has a dual nature. She is often prayed to by the sick. She may give them the healing they desire and thus exhibit her kind side or she may withhold healing and thus exhibit the destructive side of her nature."

The streets seemed to grow narrower and the bright cloth banners that Jess had noticed the previous afternoon grew more numerous.

"This is Chinatown," announced the driver. "If you like Chinese food there are many good restaurants here. I like a simple little place called Tengs. If you are very rich, you may want to try the Empress Menu at the Dragon Palace. Several years ago it cost $1800.00 per table. Probably it is more now."

Jess shook her head. "I do not like to eat that well," she said. The thought of such extravagance brought Thorpe to mind and her stomach lurched. "How much further to the office?"

"Not far, miss. The whole island is only twenty-six miles across. We'll be there in a few minutes."

True to his word in just a few minutes the driver pulled up in front of a large impressive building of glass and concrete. "Mr. Thorpe has the office on the penthouse floor," said the driver as he opened the door. "Take the express elevator."

"Thank you," she said. "And thank you for telling me about the city."

"The city and its history are important to me. They inform my poetry with meaning."

In a moment he was back in the car and driving away. Jess grew suddenly aware that she was standing in oppressive heat. It seemed to be reflected back to her from the concrete. She realized with a start that she had stepped from air conditioned house to air conditioned car so quickly that she had not even been aware of the heat on the mountain. Already she was taking luxury for granted!

She took a deep breath, clutched her shoulder bag, and pushed her way through the revolving doors.

The lobby was every bit as impressive as the outside of the building, reminding Jess, in its marbled splendor, of a great old bank lobby at home. She began to feel uncomfortable in her khaki pants. But there was nothing to do about it now. So she walked resolutely into the elevator.

When she left it a few minutes later, she almost gasped aloud. The nineteenth floor was paneled—in teakwood of course. It was air conditioned, too, and Jess welcomed its coolness. The few brief moments in the heat and humidity seemed to have sapped her strength. She breathed deeply of the cool air and approached an attractive young woman who sat at a large desk.

"I am Jess Stanton," she said. "Mr. Thorpe is expecting me."

As the woman raised her eyes from her work, Jess realized that this girl, too, was Eurasian. Her skin was a lovely ivory color. Her eyes and her hair were both jet black and she·was quite a striking figure in her red cheongsam as she rose and came around the desk. She had a figure, thought Jess, to match the rest of her.

"So you are the photographer." The tone was noncommittal enough, but the gleaming black eyes were disdainful. It was obvious that Jess had not made much of an impression.

"I am Helen Cheong, Mr. Thorpe's private secretary. I will tell him you are here."

Miss Cheong moved off, the side slit of her cheongsam revealing a long lovely leg. Well, thought Jess, this put a new complexion on things. From the way she had said 'private,' Jess could only assume that the lovely Eurasian's duties included those not usually taught in secretarial school.

She was debating with herself as to whether or not to take a seat on one of the upholstered velvet chairs that lined the paneled walls when Helen Cheong returned.

"Follow me," she said and led the way through a door into an inner office.

As she followed, Jess could not help noticing the opulence of the furnishings around her. Her feet sank deep into the dark orange carpet and the walls in here were also paneled in teak. Thorpe evidently favored that kind of wood. Another great teakwood table graced the center of this room, and, surprisingly to Jess, it was round. Somehow she had formed a mental picture of Thorpe at the head of a great table, lording it over his subordinates. This thinking, she realized, was foolishness. Those things around her were only trappings. Thorpe really had no need of them. His very presence was enough.

As she entered the two men half rose. "Come in, Jess. We're waiting for you."

Again there was that something in Thorpe's tone; Jess could not exactly put a finger on it. She was not sure whether he was laughing at her, or teasing her, or if this was his habitual tone with women.

She nodded. "The drive in was quite interesting. Singapore is an intriguing city."

Harrington nodded, but Thorpe's brows came together in a frown. "There will be time for shopping and sightseeing after we return," he said rather sharply. "Right now we have work to do."

"I am quite aware of that," Jess replied crisply. "I have no intentions of going shopping or sightseeing."

"Good. Now sit down. Lunch will be up shortly. In the meantime where's your list?"

Jess took a chair and dug the list out of her bag. "Here."

Thorpe read for some moments in silence while Jess continued to survey the room. A painting on the opposite wall, done in rich shades of orange and brown, caught her eye and she tried to make out the signature but was unsuccessful.

Another wall featured blown-up glossy prints and showed a man standing beside various flowers. The man Jess recognized as a younger, but just as handsome, Thorpe. And then the size of the flower struck her. The thing was the size of a washtub!

She sent a questioning glance at Harrington whose lips mouthed the word Rafflesia. Well, thought Jess, if they were looking for a flower of that size, they certainly wouldn't miss it.

Thorpe cleared his throat. "I propose a trip of two weeks, no longer. This amount of film seems rather excessive."

"I expect to take extra shots," returned Jess defensively.

"And where is your darkroom equipment?"

"I've listed that separately." She wished she could feel more at ease around him. It was ridiculous to be so uptight. "Conditions in the jungle are not conducive to setting up a good darkroom. It's better to wait till we return to Singapore."

She paused, but he said nothing. "I've listed some waterproof tins to store the film in. That should protect it from dampness and insects."

Thorpe eyed her sharply. "I would prefer to have the film developed in the field."

She saw Harrington give him a strange look, but she didn't wait for him to speak. "So would I, Mr. Thorpe, but that's really not sensible. Not only would there be extra equipment to carry, but the finished prints would be more difficult to protect."

Thorpe looked about to protest again when Harrington intervened. "She's right, Derek. Better to do that kind of thing when we return."

Jess gave him a grateful look. She had a feeling that Dick Harrington was going to be a big help to her on this expedition.

Thorpe conceded this point, but then he picked up on something else. By the time the lunch arrived, served by the sloe-eyed Helen Cheong swaying so seductively in her tight cheongsam that Jess yearned to stick out a foot and trip her, Jess was fuming. She knew—as well as she knew her own name—that Thorpe would never dare treat a male photographer like this. He was forcing her to defend every item on the list, as though she were some little amateur who had never seen a camera before! But she forced herself to reply calmly and evenly. Thorpe wasn't going to pressure her into doing something rash that would give him an excuse to get rid of her.

Thorpe seemed to call a moratorium on discussing the list while they ate and so Jess asked, "How do we get to where the Rafflesia grow?"

"We'll fly across the China sea in my Learjet to Kuching, the capital of Sarawak. We'll visit some Land Dyaks and then fly to Sibu at the mouth of Rajan River and take a speedboat to visit some Sea Dyaks—old friends of mine. Later we'll fly to Sabah's capital and then on to Kota Belud by land rover. We're to meet the guide there. Then it's into the jungle near Mt. Kanabalu. There's supposed to be a rare species of nepenthes there. I want to get a specimen."

"Nepenthes?" repeated Jess.

"It's also called the pitcher plant," explained

Harrington. "The bottom of the pitcher contains a sweet, sticky liquid. Insects fall in and can't get out. They die there."

"The liquid seems to have a narcotic effect," said Thorpe. "It quickly tranquilizes the victims. Hence the name nepenthes—forgetfulness."

Jess nodded. "It will be a treat to be after something that can't run away."

Harrington smiled, but Thorpe's expression remained serious. "Before we are finished you may wish yourself back in the States," he said. "The rain forest is not like the wilderness you know. It's always hot and sticky, with a humid oppressive heat that makes it difficult to breath. Even the State Park at Kinabula is no Yellowstone. The accommodations there are rough and the literature specifically warns about leeches."

"Mr. Thorpe, I have repeatedly assured you, I can handle anything that a man can. The American northwest wilderness may not be a rain forest, but it *is* a wilderness. I will take the best photos you've ever seen. There's no need at all for you to worry."

Thorpe still did not smile. "That's easy for you to *say*."

Jess bit her bottom lip. The man was impossible. She decided that silence would be her best defense and returned her attention to the lunch—a delicious chicken salad served with what could only be homemade biscuits.

The rest of the afternoon passed in much the same way with Thorpe questioning, Jess defending, and Harrington trying unsuccessfully to serve as a mediator.

Finally Thorpe reached the bottom of the list and Jess heaved a sigh of relief. It was bad enough to have Thorpe interrogating her, but the presence of Helen

Cheong, who after the lunch had been removed, remained in the room, was a constant irritant to her.

Jess could not help noticing—as she was sure the other woman meant her to—how often Helen's red-laquered fingernails rested on Thorpe's shoulders. Against his white silk shirt they stood out starkly.

There was no denying, thought Jess, that Helen Cheong was a beautiful woman, and not in the cold marble-statue way of Miss Phillips, but with a warm passionate sensuality. If this was what Thorpe meant by a warm feminine partner, then Jess could see his point. Surely any man would be taken by the ivory skin, the jet black hair, the full red lips, the voluptuous grace of the Eurasian girl. She did not like Helen Cheong, Jess thought wearily, but she was definitely the most beautiful woman she had seen in a long time.

"Now," said Thorpe. "I have an important client to see. Perhaps you can fill Jess in on anything else, Dick. And when I'm through with this Cooper woman we'll drive home together."

Jess and Harrington nodded. She could not help watching Thorpe as he made his way to the door. Yes, she thought, she had been right. He moved with the grace of a great mountain cat.

Then he was gone and she felt the tension going too.

"You look worn out," said Harrington. "Let's go sit in the corner there. We needn't talk if you're too tired."

Jess made her way to a velvet divan and sank onto it with a sigh. "I don't know why he has to make it so difficult. I'm a perfectly competent photographer. He needn't treat me like I'm a child."

Harrington smiled. "I still don't understand how you got him to change his mind." He shook his head. "I've never been able to do that."

Jess did not return the smile. "I suppose he had his

reasons—whatever they were. But I doubt that *I* had much to do with the change. It was probably some nefarious idea that occurred to him."

Harrington grinned, but he looked uncomfortable. "Don't be too hard on Derek. After all, you do have the assignment."

Jess shrugged. "Yes, I do. But he makes me so angry."

"He's not used to dealing with women." Jess raised an unbelieving eyebrow and Harrington flushed. "I mean as equals," he amended. "Usually when Derek talks to a woman she listens."

"And gives thanks for being noticed by the great man," replied Jess sharply.

"Something like that," admitted Harrington. "But they don't seem to mind."

"Well, I do," retorted Jess. "I mind a lot. I'm not used to being treated like a child. I don't like it."

"That's quite apparent." Harrington looked uneasy. "If I were you, I'd try to tone it down a bit. I mean, after all, Derek *is* the boss. It's his money that finances the expedition."

"And pays my fee," said Jess contritely. "I know it. It's just that he seems to infuriate me."

Harrington regarded her carefully. "That's rather an unusual attitude. Usually Derek—" He stopped suddenly.

"Usually he charms the women." Jess finished for him. "Isn't that what you were going to say?"

Harrington nodded. "But that seems to make you angry, too."

This was nearer the truth than Jess wanted anyone to get and she tried to change the subject. "I'm not my usual self. I guess it's jet lag catching up to me."

"Perhaps." Harrington did not seem to believe this explanation, but he did not contradict her.

Jess sighed. "I hope I have time to see something of the city."

"Are you busy tomorrow afternoon?" asked Harrington.

Jess shook her head. "No, not unless Thorpe calls a meeting."

"He won't do that," said Harrington with a smile. "I happen to know he has a big legal conference in the afternoon. So, since you're free, will you let me show you something of the city?"

Jess smiled. "I'd like that."

"I'll pick you up around two."

"Fine." Jess was conscious of a change in the relationship between them. This was obviously a date and the way Harrington looked at her indicated that he was doing more than acting on simple kindness.

"Where will we go?" she asked.

"We'll just play it by ear. Though I do want to show you the Botanic Gardens. Derek has contributed many specimens to the Gardens."

"I would like to see those," said Jess, careful to keep the anger out of her voice. "But I'd mostly like to have some fun sightseeing."

"You will," he promised.

They were smiling at each other when the door opened to admit Thorpe. "All finished," he said, eyeing them closely. "Let's go."

Jess and Harrington rose obediently. At the door Harrington turned. "I'll see you both later. Goodbye."

"Bye." Jess watched him go with real regret. His presence served as a sort of buffer. When he was there, she felt a little less in awe of Thorpe.

Thorpe said nothing as they crossed to the elevator. Helen Cheong was no longer at her desk. Probably she, too, had gone home.

The ride down to the lobby was made in silence, and,

as she followed him across its marble vastness, Jess made a face. She felt like some primitive female, walking behind her lord and master.

The car was waiting for them at the curb, but even so she felt the heat rise up from the pavement. Almost like a living thing it struck at her. Then she was seated in the air conditioned coolness and Thorpe settled beside her.

He still had said nothing and Jess felt a tension in the air. Certainly he was not going to maintain this silence all the way home. Resolutely she kept from looking at him and tried to enjoy the sights of the city passing before her window.

But finally she could bear the silence no longer and took a quick look in his direction. To her surprise she saw that he was leaning back in the seat, his eyes closed. Of course. She turned her attention back to the city. After a long day at the office, Thorpe used this time to relax and recover his energy. That was probably how he managed to do so much. From what she had seen of that office, Thorpe must be the driving force behind the whole thing.

Now that she knew he was resting, Jess felt some of her tension go. She did not, however, venture to ask the driver any questions. She simply took in the sights as they passed.

Just before they reached the driveway to the house, Thorpe straightened. "I hope Henri has something substantial for dinner. I could eat a horse."

His tone was entirely pleasant and conversational and Jess covered her surprise and answered, "The French are such notable cooks, perhaps Henri could even do something with a horse."

Thorpe chuckled and Jess felt rewarded for her effort to be nice. "At least you have a sense of humor," he said. "I hope it holds up while we're in the jungle."

"It will." Jess tried to force herself to speak lightly, but she heard the anger in her voice. He was going to persist in seeing her as inefficient until she had *proved* him wrong.

He seemed to be entirely unaware that he had ruffled her feathers. And then he turned and she saw from his eyes that he knew what he had done. And *meant* to do it.

"Dinner's at seven. See you then, kitten." He gave her a devilish grin and went striding off down the hall before she could reply.

Well, thought Jess, as she made her way to her room, one thing was certain. Derek Thorpe had charm. She should be very angry at his use of the playful nickname kitten. There was a certain patronizing quality about it. Intellectually she resented that. But emotionally some perverse part of her was quite pleased because Derek Thorpe had given her an intimate nickname.

She sighed as she took peach pants and a paler peach shirt out of the closet. She might as well recognize the inevitable. While she was working for Derek Thorpe, she was not going to be her usual normal self. But that did not mean that she would forget all her resolves. Derek Thorpe was going to learn that all women would not fall into his hands like ripe fruit. Not Jess Stanton, at least.

She had this resolve quite firmly in mind as she made her way to the dining room later. He could call her kitten all he liked; it wasn't going to get him anywhere.

The dinner did not go well. Thorpe seemed preoccupied and spoke little. Jess, still sitting on some anger from the afternoon, ate without much regard for the celebrated dish that Henri had cooked up—veal sautéed in wine. She was having a debate with herself over Derek Thorpe. After her experience in the car, she could not tell if he was deliberately ignoring her or if something was really on his mind. She hoped, if he did decide to be sociable, not to overflow with anger. But she was not quite sure she would be able to manage it.

Thorpe finished his melon at the same time she did and turned to her. "The night is still young. We might walk for a while in the garden." His eyes gleamed. "It's good for the digestion. And you can see the lights of the city."

Jess knew she should plead tiredness, jet lag, anything to avoid being alone with this man who so attracted her, but she knew, too, that she would not refuse him.

He had changed from his white suit and shirt and was wearing light trousers and a shirt of dusty pink silk. All his shirts must be silk, Jess thought, suddenly recalling the silk sheets of her bed and flushing.

"All right, let's walk," she said. If he was going to be cordial and polite, she would do her best to be the same.

At the French doors he turned to her. The soft lights of the dining room glowed in the rosy folds of his shirt and made his smile seem dark and mysterious. For a moment she wanted to turn and run. Derek Thorpe looked far too dangerous.

But she was not going to give him that satisfaction. She moved unsteadily toward him.

"The garden is beautiful this time of night," he said, slipping his hand familiarly around her elbow. A shiver went over Jess at his touch. She hoped with some embarrassment that he had not felt it.

Then he was solicitiously helping her step onto the veranda and down into the garden. The night air was heavy with the fragrance of tropical flowers. Jess sniffed appreciatively. "It's so lovely here."

"Yes, it is." Though they had reached the grass some time before, his hand still cupped her elbow, and she made no effort to avoid it.

As they moved slowly among the flowers and along the terraces, Jess felt a certain sense of peace. If only Thorpe didn't criticize her for a while, she could really enjoy this walk.

"How did you become interested in the jungle flowers?" she asked.

"I needed an avocation. The law can be all-consuming. I didn't want that to happen to me." There was a certain bitterness in his voice that surprised her. "A man needs to have balanced interests. His work, his hobbies, his play." His hand slid down to take hers and Jess, remembering her room, swallowed over the sudden lump in her throat.

"Take you, for instance." He stopped beside the small stone bench that she had used the night before. At his gesture she sat and he settled himself beside her.

"What about me?" asked Jess, knowing that she was doing as he wanted, but curious as to what he would say.

"Your life isn't balanced." In the moonlight Thorpe's smile looked even more inviting. He picked up one of her hands and began to trace patterns in her palm. "You work too hard. And don't play at all."

Jess, her body betraying her by a longing to be in his arms, tried to withdraw her hand, but he kept it captive. "My career is important to me," she said, aware that the words sounded stilted.

"Why?"

For a moment Jess was taken aback. She had never considered the why of it. "I love my work. I love to shoot pictures. Ever since I can remember, I've loved to take pictures."

"But you needn't cut yourself off from normal human experience," he said, resuming his tracing in her palm.

"I haven't." Jess was aware that her breath was coming faster.

"Yes, you have." His tone brooked no contradiction and she offered none. In the moonlight his eyes were no longer cold. Warm fires seemed to dance in them. Jess stared, fascinated in spite of herself.

"Have you ever considered that experience might enhance your art?"

Jess shook her head. "I've been making my way in my field. Besides, I have had experience."

"Not the kind I'm talking about," he said, his voice becoming even deeper.

He released her hand and reached out to touch her cheek. "You're a beautiful girl, Jess. Very beautiful."

Her skin where his finger had touched it seemed to burn and she shook her head. "I'm a woman and I'm not beautiful. You forget that I have a mirror."

He smiled, a dark mysterious smile that did strange things to her insides. "*You* forget, kitten, that *I* am a man. One of the best judges of female beauty in the city. I did not call you a girl out of some male chauvinist prejudice, but simply because you *are* a girl. The woman in you remains to be wakened."

"Mr. Thorpe—"

"Derek," he said in that deep vibrant voice.

"Mr. Thorpe," she repeated. "Whether or not the woman in me has been awakened is irrelevant—and none of your business." She wanted to make her voice cold and hard, but instead she sounded like a shocked little girl.

"When you work for me, Jess," he said softly, intimately, "everything about you is my business."

For a moment Jess sought for the right words to

retort to him, but none would come. Thorpe's arm went around her shoulder so smoothly and easily that for a moment she was tempted to nestle against him. But suddenly a picture of the seductive Helen Cheong flashed into her mind. Jess stiffened, but she did not want to offend him any further, after all, she still did want the job. Desperately she sought for another subject of conversation.

"You have some very interesting employees," she stammered.

He gave her a quizzical look, but she hurried on. "I talked to Ah Cheng and her husband this morning. She thinks you are the world's greatest person."

Thorpe grinned. "Ah Cheng is biased. She practically raised me and she looks upon me as her own."

"It is kind of you to keep them on."

His face hardened. "I am not quite the monster you suppose me to be. But to keep in character for you I might suggest that Ah Cheng and Giok Leng are very dependable. Much more so than the young people one hires these days."

Jess flushed. She had been rude again, it seemed. Surely she had not meant to and yet she *had* had that sort of image of him—a man who was without the better feelings. "I'm sorry," she mumbled. "I didn't mean to offend you. I like Ah Cheng very much."

"So do I," said Thorpe, his voice softening. "I also have a driver who writes haikus."

"You know?" In spite of herself she could not help being surprised.

"Of course I know. I make it my business to know. Besides, Lee's poetry isn't bad. He's even gotten some published."

Jess was silent. There was a great deal more to Thorpe than she had imagined.

His hand came to rest lightly on her shoulder and

again she fought to keep from leaning against him. She would have to go in, she told herself firmly. This was getting far too dangerous.

She stirred on the bench. "I really must be getting to bed," she said. "Ah Cheng expects me for breakfast early. She has promised me pancakes."

Thorpe smiled. "You will enjoy them, I guarantee it." He got to his feet and pulled her up, too. They were extremely close and Jess felt her heart begin to pound again.

"And now," he said, "since jet lag has obviously caught up with you, I'll send you off to bed. But first, just let me show you one point where the view of the city's lights is tremendous." And he took her hand with such ease that she did not even think of withdrawing it.

Moments later they stood side by side, looking out toward the city. The radiance of the lights gave a strange glow to the sky above it and Jess took a deep breath. "What a shot that would make! Civilization can be quite beautiful sometimes."

"Yes, it can," Thorpe agreed. "But I suppose I prefer the wilderness. Life is clearer there, closer to the basics, not complicated by a lot of unnatural needs and desires."

Well, thought Jess, Thorpe was a philosopher, too. "Yes, the wilderness is like that. Raw and unspoiled. And I love it. But there's one part of civilization that I always miss."

"And that is?"

"The bathtub." Jess thought suddenly of the luxurious tub that adjoined her room and flushed again. But fortunately it was too dark for him to see.

Thorpe laughed. "Just like a woman," he said.

Jess was nettled. "There's nothing wrong with being clean," she said as he led her back toward the house.

He took her to the veranda outside her room before

he answered. Then he put his hands on her shoulders and turned her to face him. Her body trembled under his touch and she thought surely he must feel it. "Of course not. You take as many baths as you like, kitten."

For a long moment his eyes held hers and she thought that surely he would repeat his kiss. Her knees went weak at the thought. And then he dropped his arms and moved swiftly away, his soft good night coming back over his shoulder.

Jess turned and opened her French doors with trembling fingers. For the realization was strong upon her. She had wanted Derek Thorpe's kiss, wanted it very badly. In spite of all her protestations to him, in spite of all her firm words to herself, she was becoming more and more attracted to the man. And the results could only be disastrous!

# Chapter 3

When Jess awoke the next morning, she felt groggy and irritable. Jet lag was a miserable business. When would her disrupted biological rhythms get themselves in order again?

But of course it had been late before she had fallen asleep. It seemed like she had spent hours tossing and turning between those silk sheets, trying to get the thought of Derek Thorpe out of her mind.

She had not succeeded, of course. But finally she had succumbed to exhaustion. And now she felt as though she had not slept at all. Still, Ah Cheng was expecting her. And this afternoon Dick Harrington would arrive for their sightseeing tour.

She sat up and swung her feet out of the bed. First she would take a nice bath. Thorpe's voice came back to her—"You take as many baths as you like, kitten." How was it possible for the man to invest something so mundane with so much intimacy? It was like he gave his personal approval to the idea. Almost as though baths would advance *his* purpose.

She was getting paranoid, Jess thought with a smile as she entered the bathroom and began to run the water. But then, perhaps Thorpe did think something like that. There *was* a certain sensuous quality to a warm bath. And hadn't the Romans, famous for their licentiousness, been very fond of baths?

She flushed suddenly as she realized that Thorpe knew about the mirrors. Perhaps he thought she was admiring herself in them when the truth of the matter was that she studiously avoided looking in them at all. Even now, still wearing her pajamas, she kept her eyes averted.

She slipped out of her pajamas and slid into the inviting water with a sigh. Decadent or not, there was nothing to compare to a nice relaxing bath. She put all thought of Thorpe and the jungle out of her mind and relaxed.

A little later, clad in slacks and shirt, she made her way to the kitchen. The little Chinese woman grinned as Jess pushed open the door. "Very good," said Ah Cheng. "You come."

Jess smiled. It was good to be so welcomed. "Yes, Ah Cheng. I have come. I want to hear about your life in China."

Ah Cheng bowed slightly. "I tell you. But you eat American pancakes?"

Jess nodded. "That'll be fine."

"Good. I cook and talk same time. When I was young," her black eyes darted a glance at Jess. "Younger than you. I live in China. In country. My family raise pigs. I work hard. Life was good."

Jess, with her ranch background could appreciate this and nodded.

"But marrying must be done. My father call the *hm̂-lâng,* the go-between. She find me a husband."

"Find?" said Jess.

Ah Cheng nodded. "Our marriage blind. No see each other first. That best way."

Jess was startled. "You never saw each other? Not once?"

"Not till wedding day. Giok Leng's mother, she

come with go-between. See if I strong. Work hard. Have many sons." A spasm of pain crossed the little woman's face.

"I look strong. She say go ahead. My family keep gifts matchmaker bring. Give her card that tells my name, hour, day, month, year of birth." The old woman grinned. "No good to give tiger woman to sheep man."

Jess frowned. "I don't understand."

"Each year, day, hour ruled by different animal. Time of borning gives name of character. Tiger eat sheep. Not good."

"Oh. I see. It's a kind of astrology."

Ah Cheng nodded. "Yes, I hear Master Derek explain that way. So, Giok Leng and me, we match all right. Then gifts sent. Wild goose and roll of silk."

Again Jess looked bewildered.

"Engagement presents. Like American girl get ring."

"Oh."

*"Phèng-kim* sent, too. Part then, rest before wedding."

"What is that?"

"Bride-price."

"He *bought* you?"

Ah Cheng smiled. "That is custom."

"In old days," added Giok Leng, who had just slipped into the room, "man could sell wife in market."

Ah Cheng nodded. "Custom show that now woman belong man's family. She work for them."

Jess found this rather startling, but said nothing more. How well Derek Thorpe would have fit into such a society!

Ah Cheng continued "Fortune tellers set good day and hour. I put on beautiful red dress and headgear."

"Red?"

"Red color of joy," explained Giok Leng.

Ah Cheng nodded. "I tell my parents goodbye and go in red sedan chair to Giok Leng's house. His people waiting. He comes and kicks chair."

"To show I am man," said Giok Leng with a grin.

"Then we go to worship ancestors, see our room, feast goes on."

Jess was full of questions. "When do your people come?"

Ah Cheng shook her head. "Don't. My people feast at my house. We go visit on third day after wedding."

"But didn't they attend the ceremony?"

"No, only bride's younger brother, sometimes."

By now Jess was realizing how little she had really considered other cultures.

"I am hair wife," said Ah Cheng proudly.

Jess smiled ruefully. "I'm afraid I'm terribly ignorant about these things. What does that mean?"

Ah Cheng touched the thick coil of black hair at her neck. "When girl marries—virgin girl—her friends put up her hair. This shows her a woman."

"I see."

"Hair wife is main wife," said Giok Leng. "She have first place. Other wives come later. They are secondary."

"Other wives?"

Giok Leng nodded. "Man may take other wives if he wish. Or concubines." He smiled at the little woman busily turning pancakes. "I no wish."

"My," said Jess. "This is all very different from an American wedding."

Ah Cheng smiled. "Yes, Chinese very different. When I go Giok Leng's house, I must obey his parents. Work for them."

"But you were a grown woman," protested Jess.

"No matter. Everyone obey the father. Giok Leng, his mother, five brothers, brothers' wives, brothers' children. All live together."

"Person not important in China," explained Giok Leng. "Family important."

"Why did you leave your home?" asked Jess as Ah Cheng set pancakes, butter, and syrup before her.

"Father go to ancestors. Elder brother head of family. Things go bad. No rain. Mother tell us go Singapore. Make money. Send home."

Ah Cheng nodded. "Money we send keep land for family. We happy."

"Do you ever want to go back to China?" asked Jess, between mouthfuls of pancakes.

Ah Cheng shook her head. "No. Singapore home now. No leave Master Derek. Things not same in China. All brothers gone to ancestors."

Jess finished up the pancakes and smiled. "Ah Cheng, you are a wonderful cook. The pancakes were perfection."

Ah Cheng beamed. "Very glad you like. I make American breakfast every morning. You eat."

"Thank you, I will."

The little woman and her husband were still bowing and smiling as Jess left the kitchen. As she made her way back to her room, Jess considered their conversation. How different it must be to be raised in another culture. The thought of a blind marriage gave her a great deal of horror. And the idea of being a main wife, of having other wives come into the household after her, was startling, to say the least.

Things in the States were not always rosy, it was true. A woman often had to work harder than a man to get any place in her career. But at least she had a chance.

In the China of Ah Cheng's girlhood a woman did as she was told. And that was that.

As she pushed open the door to her room, Jess had a sudden fantasy. There was Derek Thorpe in traditional Chinese garb and behind him a long line of women. The first was the tall and stately Haviland Phillips, her cool blond beauty set off by a jade green cheongsam. Behind her stood the seductively smiling Helen Cheong in a startling red cheongsam that fit like a second skin. The third woman in the line had a mop of curly red hair and instead of wearing a sultry cheongsam was clad in the shapeless black trousers and blue blouse of the coolie.

Jess snorted and slammed the door behind her. She would never be number three on Derek Thorpe's list of women. Never! When she loved, she intended it to be in the traditional sense, traditional *American* sense, she amended, of one man and one woman. When she loved, she intended for it to end in marriage.

With a sigh she threw herself on the bed. Everything she did and everything she thought seemed colored by Derek Thorpe's entrance into her life. Once things had been quite clear and simple. Now, nothing was clear.

She was even becoming unsure about things that before had been second nature to her. She knew quite well that the green filter was the one to use when shooting flowers. Certainly it stood to reason. Since a filter eliminated its own color a green filter would cut out the green shadows that the foliage cast. She knew this as well as she knew her own name. Yet she persisted in worrying about it. What if it didn't work? What if all the pictures came out poorly or—didn't come out at all?

Jess rolled over onto her side and searched in the drawer of the bedside table for her photography book.

Old and tattered, it showed the effects of much use. But she had learned a great deal from it and she never went into the field without it. It was rather like having an old friend along.

She sighed again and turned to the section on filters.

By the time she had finished the chapter she had calmed her fears about the filter. She had been right about using the green one. She knew everything the book had to say about filters. There was no reason for anything to go wrong. No reason at all. And if it did—

Jess dropped the book and jumped to her feet. The picture of an angry Derek Thorpe—angry with her— was almost more than she could bear.

She glanced at her watch. Dick Harrington would be there soon. She had better get ready. What a pleasure it would be to spend some time with a man without having her nerves strung taut and ready to snap.

She opened the closet door. Her eyes lingered on the green sundress and she was about to reach for it, but the memory of what had happened the last time she wore it, the memory of Thorpe's kiss, made her change her mind. She would not wear the green dress; she reached for a pair of green slacks and a cream-colored blouse instead, though she knew that nothing would make her forget Thorpe's kiss. Nothing.

She moved restlessly toward the bathroom and then stopped, Thorpe's words about baths were coming back to her again. Jess threw up her hands in despair. There was no way of escaping the man; his presence was everywhere, a haunting reminder of what she had given up in pursuing her career. Except, she told herself defiantly, she had never really given up anything. For she had never had a man like Thorpe and so could not have given him up. Nor would she, she told herself, if he were hers, let anything get in the way of their love.

"Dear God!" said Jess aloud as she realized what she was thinking. She must have lost her mind! Nothing had ever interfered with her passion for photography and now she was admitting that a man—and a man to whom she was nothing more than a plaything—meant more to her than her career.

"I've had it," said Jess. "I've got to stop this. I've got to."

She stopped and glared at herself defiantly in the mirror. And then she had to laugh. She looked like she was ready to rip someone apart! If this was love, she told herself ruefully, it was even more painful than the poets said. But it couldn't be love. It was just some chemical attraction. Thorpe attracted women like—like poison attracted rats, she thought with a grimace of distaste. And he was just as deadly.

She picked up the brush and began to brush her unruly curls. They wouldn't look much different when she was done, but she would have the satisfaction of knowing they had been brushed.

The phone rang and Jess started. She was certainly a bundle of nerves. "Hello?"

"Mr. Harrington here with car," said Ah Cheng's soft voice.

"Fine. I'll be right out."

Jess replaced the receiver and took up her purse. She supposed she was ready. Her sandals were not highheeled and glamorous, being made for comfort rather than fashion, but she was satisfied that she would finish the afternoon in good walking shape.

As she made her way toward the front foyer, she wondered how the afternoon would go. She was not accustomed to dealing with men on a purely social basis and so she felt a little uneasy. On the other hand, Harrington was quite friendly and easygoing and, if he did not insist on talking about Thorpe, all should go well.

"Hello. You're looking fine."

"Thank you. You're not looking so bad yourself." His suit was well-cut and obviously expensive, and yet Jess was aware that it lacked a certain something that seemed to characterize Thorpe's clothes.

"I thought first we'd go to the Botanic Gardens," he grinned. "Then, with duty disposed of, we can just have fun."

"Sounds great," said Jess. "Lead on."

When they reached the Gardens, Jess looked around. "I really do like flowers, Dick. But if we look at all this—"

He grinned. "I just want to show you the specimens that Derek brought in."

Jess followed dutifully. "But tell me, what makes *you* go out in the jungle after flowers?"

Harrington looked embarrassed, but finally he answered, "Derek."

Jess frowned. "I don't understand."

"Derek is my friend," Harrington explained. "These trips are vitally important to him."

Jess was confused. "But he told me— He said this was just an avocation. Something to balance his life."

Harrington shook his head. "Whatever Derek does he does completely and absolutely. When he's in the courtroom, it's just unbelievable. He's so single-minded. And in the jungle he's the same way."

"But that doesn't explain *your* involvement," she insisted.

"Derek has—" He hesitated as though unwilling to go on.

"Tell me."

"Well, Derek has few close friends. He's hardhitting and aggressive. And in his position of power—"

"In other words, you're the only man willing to go with him," said Jess.

"Well—"

"Come on, that's the truth, isn't it?" she persisted.

"Yes, but you're being unfair. It's not Derek's fault. He's always been like that. Driven by some inner need to be the best at everything he undertakes."

"I see." By this time they had reached the Rafflesia. Even though it wasn't in bloom, Jess regarded the huge plant with awe.

Then Harrington took her hand and led her to another exhibit. "Here's the pitcher plant we brought back last year, Nepenthes Thorpea." He watched her closely.

Jess managed a small smile and then she asked pointedly, "Where are the plants named after you?"

Harrington looked embarrassed. "There are none."

"But you were there, too!"

"Jess, I just went along for the ride. Don't make me out a victim. Derek paid all the expenses and did all the work."

"And I suppose a trek into the rain forest is your idea of a fun vacation!"

He smiled. "Of course not. It's quite hard physical work. But I enjoy it and it helps keep me fit. Now, for heaven's sake, let's quite wrangling over Derek. I want to show you the city. We won't mention him again. Agreed?"

Jess nodded. "Agreed."

They drove for a while and then Dick said, "We'll walk from here. It's easier to see things."

Jess nodded. Soon they were standing on the sidewalk beneath a huge poster of a Chinese girl with a powdered white face and long black hair hanging free to her waist. With a great sword she was keeping off a number of villainous looking men. Jess sent Harrington a quizzical look.

"Ad for a Chinese movie," he explained. "Quite a woman, isn't she?"

Jess nodded. "But why is *she* fighting the villains?"

Harrington grinned. "She's the heroine, a descendant of the *tao-ma-tan* literally saber-steed *tan,* of the classic Chinese theater. She was a fighting princess or a woman bandit, something like that. On the stage such an actor—"

"Actor?" said Jess.

"Yes. The women were forbidden to be on the stage by an old Imperial decree and so female impersonators played their roles, the *tan* roles."

"But this is obviously a woman."

He nodded. "Actresses made a comeback after the Revolution of 1911. Still, she carries the tradition with her."

"Isn't there a hero?" asked Jess.

Harrington shrugged. "Probably not. She's the star. She does all the fighting and cleansing of the earth of wickedness, sort of a female Errol Flynn."

Jess grinned. "Why is her face powdered?"

"That's a vestige of the classical theater, too," Harrington replied. "Part of the traditional makeup. I wish it was later in the year. You'd enjoy a Chinese street opera. Usually there are quite a few around the fifteenth day of the seventh moon, the Feast of the Hungry Ghosts."

Jess shuddered. "It sounds like a title for a bad horror movie."

"Once a year the ghosts of the dead are let out of purgatory. There will be great tables of food set up for them."

"For ghosts?"

Harrington nodded. "Later in the day the people will eat what's left. They say there's no flavor to it then."

"Are you trying to scare me?" Jess asked with a nervous grin.

Harrington smiled. "No, I'm not. Speaking of food reminds me that it's lunch time. Have you eaten?"

"No."

"Good. We'll have *satay*. You can't leave Singapore without trying *satay*."

It wasn't very long till Jess was biting at the little chunks of crisp roasted meat on a stick, watching the Malay fan the flames of his charcoal burner as he prepared to cook more.

Rather cautiously Jess asked, "What kind of meat is this?"

"Chicken, beef, and mutton," Harrington answered. "Relax. No chocolate covered ants, etc."

The meat was delicious Jess admitted as she chewed on it and the slices of cucumber that accompanied it. She had been hungry, very hungry.

They demolished several more sticks each, Harrington being careful to hold onto all the empty sticks. When he handed them to the Malay who solemnly counted them, Jess understood. This was how a person reckoned his tab. No check—just a handful of sticks.

Harrington smiled at her. "Let's take a trishaw to the Thieves' Market. You'll like it there." He led her to the side of the road where brown-skinned men sat with their strange-looking vehicles. "We are going to Thieves' Market," he said, singling out one.

The driver nodded and stood by while Harrington helped Jess into the seat. It was rather like a motorcycle sidecar, only roomier. The back of the bicycle was attached to one wheel of the cart and the other side had a wheel of its own. Harrington climbed in beside her and they set off.

Before long the trishaw had stopped and Harrington was helping her out. "Here it is. The Thieves' Market. They used to say that if you were robbed in the night you could come here in the morning and buy your stuff back for one-third its original price."

Jess looked at him in surprise.

"That was in the old days. The city's very law-abiding now. Why, you can be fined for dropping a cigarette butt on the street. And you will be."

Jess nodded. "Yes, I know. Fortunately I don't smoke."

Harrington chuckled as they wandered on. Here was a cubbyhole full of nothing but pots and pans, some so battered it was doubtful that they would hold water. There a painter was displaying portraits of important people. A heavily bearded Sikh stood with folded arms before a display of brass. An old Indian crouched behind heaps of used clothes. A Chinese boy chanted the charms of a motorcycle to a bemused youth.

Jess was fascinated by the endless rows of curios and knickknacks. Fat Chinese Buddhas of many sizes and colors contemplated their navels. Brilliant porcelain eggs nestled in their brass cups. A white-bearded god with a strange high forehead and bushy white eyebrows stared at her. Glassware of every kind glittered in the sun.

Her eye was caught by an ivory statue of a nude lady. "How different," she said to Harrington. The lady had little of the look of nakedness about her, yet she was undeniably without clothes.

Harrington, following her pointed finger, laughed. "Some of these are real antiques. The Chinese doctors used them. They had their patients point out where it hurt."

"On a statue?"

"Of course. Chinese ladies were very modest. They couldn't point out things on their own bodies. In fact, the doctor couldn't touch them either."

Jess smiled. "The poor ladies must have had a rough time of it."

"I suppose they did. Listen, I'm going to buy it. Watch an expert in action."

Jess watched for fifteen minutes as Harrington and the wizened little proprietor of the stall bargained, grimacing and practically insulting each other. Finally Harrington emerged victorious and put a package in her hand. "Here—a souvenir of our city."

Jess flushed. "Oh, Dick, you shouldn't have."

"Nonsense. I wanted to and I did. Now, let's move along."

Jess tucked the package into her bag. She was really very pleased at the gift; it would certainly make a good conversation piece at home. But she was a little uneasy about it, too. She did not want Dick Harrington to get any ideas about her.

A high, thin, reedy sound came through the noises of the market. Harrington grabbed her arm. "Good. A snake charmer. Come on."

Jess followed him as he hurried through the crowd, then came to a sudden halt. Sitting cross-legged before a woven basket, a gaunt emaciated Indian blew on some sort of wind instrument. As the cobra's head rose above the basket, Jess drew a deep breath. Snakes were not her favorite creatures. It was evidently a big snake, what was called a spectacled cobra, she thought. Its wide-spread hood disclosed weird markings that looked very much like a death's-head. Jess couldn't quite suppress a shiver. The cobra looked dangerous and she knew from experience that venomous snakes, whether cobras or rattlers, were nothing to mess around with. A slight hissing sound issued from the snake as it swayed in time to the Indian's music. The narrow black tongue flicked in and out, the beady eyes glistening as it surveyed the crowd.

Harrington turned to her. "No need to worry. The snake charmer has removed the fangs."

"No doubt," said Jess. "I'm not worried. I was born and raised in rattler country, Dick. I know what snakes look like."

Harrington nodded. "That's good because we may just see some."

Jess contented herself with a nod. If Harrington started doubting her, she would just scream, she told herself.

"I want you to see The Tiger Balm Garden and The House of Jade," he said as they left the snake charmer behind. "They were both started by Aw Boon Haw, The Tiger Balm King and his brother, Aw Boon Par. They made their fortune from Tiger Balm and Tiger Oil."

"What are they?" asked Jess.

Harrington shook his head. "No one knows the exact ingredients. The Chinese use them for everything. Have for the last fifty years. The House of Jade is a fabulous collection. It includes pieces from every important dynasty in China. There are also Chinese paintings—delightful to look at in their delicacy."

"Tell me about the Garden," said Jess.

"It's also called Haw Par Villa. It overlooks the sea at Pasir Panjang. Hillside land has been carved into grottos, caves and paths, and studded with weird and wonderful recreations from Chinese mythology. Some scenes are happy ones, some are warnings in the form of allegories, and some—" He grinned. "Some are very graphic presentations of rather lurid tortures."

Jess grinned, too. "I think I can handle that."

Harrington glanced at his watch. "Well, probably we'd better let the Garden go for today. The House of Jade is closer and I want to stop at the Dragon Palace for dinner."

"The Dragon Palace," repeated Jess as Harrington summoned a cab. "I know. That's the one Lee the chauffeur mentioned."

The House of Jade was just as fabulous as Harrington had said. They wandered from display to display, marveling at the artistry. Finally he said, "My stomach says it's dinner time. How about yours?"

Jess nodded.

"Then it's off to the Cockpit Hotel and The Dragon Palace Restaurant."

To her surprise Jess found the car waiting for them outside. "I believe in being prepared," Harrington said with a smile. "Besides, it's more difficult to get a cab out here."

It didn't take long to get to the restaurant and soon Jess was seated by a graceful Chinese girl in a modest cheongsam.

"What'll you have?" asked Harrington.

Jess shook her head. "You choose for me. The only Chinese food I've ever had was chop suey and chow mein. And fortune cookies."

"We'll start off with birds' nest soup and then *moo goo gai pan* for the lady and roast duckling for me."

He turned to Jess with a smile. "The duckling is cooked in a ginger sauce. You can sample mine."

Jess nodded and looked around the lavish room. The walls were decorated with great painted dragons and graceful Chinese lanterns shed their soft light on the tables. "I'm feeling a little uncomfortable," she admitted.

"Whatever for?"

"This is a place for the likes of Haviland Phillips," she said ruefully.

Harrington shook his head. "You're wrong. After an afternoon like we've had—*if* she'd ever consent to it—Haviland would be wilted. You still look fresh as a daisy."

Jess smiled. "Thank you, sir. You make lovely compliments."

His hand covered hers. "It's the truth," he said. "Besides, Haviland isn't even a woman."

Jess looked at him in surprise, as she carefully withdrew her fingers.

"Oh, she looks sophisticated enough, but she's really just a spoiled little girl who wants her own way. Thanks to her Daddy and his money she's always gotten it."

"She wants Thorpe," said Jess and then was appalled at her frankness.

Harrington didn't seem at all surprised. "Yes, she does. And I suppose we can't blame her. Most women do."

Jess had no reply for this and he continued. "Derek may even marry her. Someday."

Jess felt her heart rise up in her throat but she kept herself from saying anything.

"Not because he loves her. I don't see how anyone can do that. But she does have a classic beauty and she'd fit well. She knows how to conduct herself socially."

"And then Helen Cheong can remain his mistress." Jess clapped a hand over her mouth. "I'm sorry. I shouldn't have said that. But neither of them has been particularly cordial to me. And Helen made her affiliation quite clear."

Harrington frowned. "I suppose Derek might do that. A lot of rich Chinese keep more than one wife and concubines, too. But I can't really see Derek marrying just yet. It's not his style."

"He really has no need to," said Jess. "As I once read in some old book, 'When a man gets his milk free, there's not much sense in buying a cow.'"

For just a moment Harrington stared at her and then he laughed. "Well, Jess, you certainly speak your mind. Our expedition this year ought to be an exciting one."

"You needn't expect any fireworks between Thorpe and me," said Jess with a rueful smile. "I intend to do my job and keep my mouth shut."

The food arrived then and their conversation turned to other matters. Jess sampled the duckling and proclaimed it delicious, relished the *moo goo gai pan,* and was not quite sure whether or not to believe Harrington's avowal that the soup was really, literally, made from birds' nests. "Cross my heart," he said. "There's a certain place where they encourage the birds to build so they can collect them."

Night had fallen when they left the hotel and settled once more in the car. In the closeness it seemed only natural for Harrington to put his arm around her shoulders. He grinned at her cheerfully as he did so and she smiled in return. It seemed stupid to evade his arm. With Dick everything was open and aboveboard. No mysterious smiles in the moonlight and enigmatic conversations about 'experience.' Unconsciously, Jess sighed.

"Getting tired?" asked Harrington, his arm tightening around her.

She shook her head. "Just a little."

He smiled at her warmly. "There's a great deal more to see, but we'll save that for another time. Okay?"

"Okay."

The weariness continued to creep over her, but she could not tell if it was caused by the day's excursion or if its origin was psychological. Surely she had spent many much more arduous days in the wilderness, on the go from dawn to dusk, and never felt this tired. It could also be jet leg. Or it could have something to do with the prospect of seeing Derek Thorpe again. Jess rather suspected that it was the latter.

"Some night soon I'd like to take you to dinner at the restaurant on Mt. Faber," he said as the car moved out of the city. "It's beautiful dining outdoors there."

"That sounds nice," said Jess, leaning back in the seat. "I'll be looking forward to it."

They said nothing more, simply sitting in companionable silence until the car pulled up in front of Thorpe's house.

Harrington stepped out and helped her. For a moment he looked down into her eyes and then he grinned and pulled her to him. "Thanks for a fun day," he said, before his lips sought hers. Jess turned her head just in time to take the kiss on her cheek.

"Thank you, Dick." Jess wished that she could draw his head down and kiss him properly, but that would not help matters. As long as she was infatuated with Derek Thorpe it would not be wise to encourage Dick. As she watched the car drive away, she asked herself ironically why she couldn't have fallen deeply and madly in love with Harrington. Now there was a man worthy of a woman's respect.

With a sigh she turned toward the house. There was no use wasting her time in such speculations. She would just go to her room, take a long, relaxing bath, and hopefully fall asleep quickly.

She pushed the doorbell and wondered if Ah Cheng had told Thorpe she was out with Dick. Not that it was any of his business.

The door opened and to her surprise Thorpe himself stood there. His shirt was open halfway down his chest, revealing crisp curly hair of the same color as that on his head. Her eyes lingered there for the barest of moments before she raised them to meet his. His eyes were cold and distant as he said, "Well, you've decided to return."

There was no doubt that he was angry, very angry, and Jess felt her own anger rising in return. She did not want to have her fun day spoiled by this arrogant man. "Of course I've returned," she said as calmly as she could. "I have a contract."

Thorpe frowned. "I didn't bring you to Singapore to have you go cavorting about the island."

"I wasn't cavorting," retorted Jess. "I was seeing the island—an entirely normal pastime for someone not born here."

"I hired you to take pictures," he said curtly.

"And what pictures did you want me to take this afternoon?" she asked with mock sweetness.

"You know what I mean."

By this time he was glaring at her and she glared back.

"I'm afraid you're mistaken, Mr. Thorpe. I understood that you hired me as the photographer for an expedition into the jungle. We have not yet left for the jungle. My equipment is ready, my lists have been turned in. There is nothing left for me to do. Unless, of course, you wished to have a meeting this afternoon. In which case you could have given me sufficient warning."

"I was in a legal conference all afternoon," he admitted gruffly.

"Then I fail to see what you have to be angry about."

"You were not here for dinner."

"I didn't realize that part of my job entailed my being here for dinner," she said crisply. "In the future please be more specific. I could hardly be expected to know that you had bought all my time."

Thorpe was still glaring at her. The muscles around his jaw tightened as he stepped closer. "You are being ridiculous," he said stiffly. "I did not buy all your time. I just expected that you would adhere to the simple rules of courtesy. Employee or houseguest, one does not simply vanish without a word. I was concerned for your safety."

"But I didn't *vanish!* And I *was* safe. I'm a grown woman, not some kind of child." She wondered if he knew she'd been with Harrington. With Thorpe in this mood she didn't want to get Dick in trouble. But she had to defend herself. "Ah Cheng knew I went out."

"Did you tell her when you would return?"

"No, but I didn't know."

This information did not seem to calm him at all and, as he continued to glare at her, Jess felt her temper rising higher. He had no right to treat her this way. No right at all. She hadn't done anything wrong. Just because she wanted to enjoy herself a little, to forget serious things for a while. His words of the night before came back to her and before she thought she blurted out, "I thought you were an advocate of experience, Mr. Thorpe."

For a moment there was a deep silence. Then, as she realized how her words could be taken, Jess flushed. She would have to put a bridle on her tongue. She had not experienced any man in the way Thorpe had insinuated and she did not want him to think that she had. Yet she knew no way to recall her hasty words or to refute them without making a bad situation worse. And still he continued to glare at her until it seemed that her body was on fire with yearning for him.

It was insane, Jess told herself, quite insane, to yearn

for a man like this. He was arrogant and condescend-ing, by far the most infuriating man she had ever known. Yet she wanted desperately to be in his arms.

"I—I'm tired," Jess said. "Goodnight."

"Not yet." There was something in his voice that made her blood race.

"Mr. Thorpe—"

"You might as well call me Derek," he said as he took another step closer. "We're in this together now, whether we like it or not."

Jess tried, but her lips would not form the words. She wanted to utter a crisp good night and march off. But she seemed rooted to the spot, charmed by the malignant power of his eyes. They were like the eyes of the cobra, she thought as her breath quickened. They held her spellbound as the snake held its victims—until it was too late.

She started to move then, but his hands were already on her. "I don't consider this thing settled at all. And I intend to speak to Harrington about it."

"It wasn't his fault," Jess said. "You mustn't blame him." Her arms where Thorpe's hands rested seemed to burn from his touch.

"He knows better," he continued, as though she had not spoken at all.

Suddenly Jess was infuriated. "Who do you think you are?" she cried. "Just because Dick was nice to me, showed me the city, you're going to yell at him. You're behaving like a spoiled brat who has to have everything his way."

Their faces were only inches apart and Jess wanted desperately to escape from him before she said any-thing else damaging. But his grip on her arms tightened and she barely stopped from gasping aloud at the pain.

"And you," he said, his voice thick with rage, "are a

spoiled little girl who thinks she knows everything. And really knows nothing at all."

For long moments they stood and then Jess began to struggle. She could no longer stand the sight of those eyes boring into hers. "Let me go," she cried and she was horrified to realize that she was close to tears.

But her struggles were useless. Not only did he refuse to let her go, he drew her slowly into his arms.

"No," she whispered. "No, you mustn't."

But he seemed to hear nothing. She was crushed against his chest, and, when she tried to turn her face away to escape him, he held it with an iron hand under her chin. Something within Jess surged like a wild thing. She wanted to escape from him and yet she didn't want to. His eyes probed deep into hers and then slowly, with a smile that was terrible to see, he bent and took her lips with his.

She tried very hard to remain cold and unyielding, but it was impossible. The pressure of his body against hers, of his mouth on hers, sent her blood racing and her senses rocketing off into ecstasy. His mouth bruised hers, punished it. She felt the hard edge of his teeth against her lip and yet she really did not want him to stop. The wild thing inside her exulted at the very savage brutality of his kiss, exulted in it and bowed to it until she seemed to have no will of her own, until she clung to him, her body melting into his.

Then, quite suddenly, he put her from him. "If it's experience you want," he said with a harsh mocking smile. "You must come to the master." And then he was gone, leaving her weak and trembling, her resolutions and her values, like so many shattered statues of saints, lying in pieces at her feet.

# Chapter 4

By morning Jess felt worn out. She had spent the night tossing and turning, debating with herself. This thing with Thorpe was getting out of hand and she didn't know what to do about it. This was the most lucrative assignment of her whole career. She didn't want to run away from it.

But after last night—Jess shivered though the room wasn't cold. Last night, as angry as she had been with him, Derek Thorpe had mastered her. He had kissed her into submission and if he had chosen to go further— She pulled the silken sheets up under her chin. She really did not know if she would have been able to stop him. His kiss had left her so weak and trembling, so full of yearning for him.

Jess rolled over and pounded the silk-encased pillow. This kind of thinking was stupid. So she had succumbed to a kiss. So what? She was human, wasn't she? And just because she had let him kiss her, that didn't mean—

She got up suddenly and went to search for some clothes. Enough of this going around in circles. She would just go and get her breakfast.

Minutes later she was with Ah Cheng in the kitchen. The little woman seemed very glad to see her and her only comment concerning the previous day was a soft, "Master Derek say you talk lunch time. Leave this afternoon for jungle."

Jess nodded. "That's fine." She felt a certain sense of compunction. If they were leaving that soon, he might well have had something legitimate to discuss with her the night before.

"Sausage with eggs today?" asked Ah Cheng and Jess nodded absently.

The Chinese woman's bright black eyes regarded her carefully. "You no sleep good. You tired."

"I guess it's jet lag," said Jess.

Ah Cheng looked wise. "Maybe so. Maybe something else."

Jess sighed. "I guess it's the whole thing about men. I don't understand them."

Ah Cheng looked surprised. "Men are men. They have their ways. We have ours."

Jess sighed again. "I don't see how you could do it," she said. "Give your whole life into a man's hands. I couldn't do that."

Ah Cheng smiled wisely. "I young. Know no other way. In China only self-combed woman do anything else. I not like that."

From Ah Cheng's expression of distaste Jess could see that such women were 'bad.' "Tell me about a self-combed woman," she said. "What does that mean?"

"Remember I tell you when girl marries, they put up her hair?"

"Yes."

"Self-combed woman no marry. Put up own hair. Take care of self. Do as she please. Bad."

"But maybe she only wants to be free."

Ah Cheng looked startled. "No good to be without family. Sometimes such women take husbands, but they not honor them. Sometimes two, three women live together."

Jess could see that Ah Cheng's opinion of such

women wasn't going to be easily changed, so she took another tack. "Do girls in Singapore still marry blind?"

"Sometime. In older, better families." Ah Cheng shook her head. "The young now think they have right to choose. Families not agree. Bad trouble. You see new tall houses people live?"

"The high-rises?"

Ah Cheng nodded. "Sometimes young lovers jump from balcony because parents say no."

Jess shivered. Once she would have seen such actions as utter foolishness. But now—with the memory of Derek Thorpe's arms and lips haunting her—she could sympathize with those who were denied their love.

"Is the Chinese wedding ceremony still the same?" she asked.

Ah Cheng smiled. "Some girls wear Western dress. Not white, pink. Depends on parents. Much stay the same. Still bride-price."

Jess frowned. In her present distraught condition she did not want to think about anything that put men in a position of authority.

Ah Cheng was silent for some time, busily turning the sputtering sausages and Jess drifted off into a fantasy in which she saw herself in red robes and headgear, waiting timidly for a groom she had never seen to come and kick her red sedan chair. And when the door was opened, Derek Thorpe stood there, ferociously handsome and oozing male power. Dear God, thought Jess. What chance would a woman have in a situation like that?

"Blind marriage best," said Ah Cheng. "People learn love and respect. Self-combed woman—" She made an eloquent face. "No good."

There was a brief pause. "You see Helen Cheong?" asked Ah Cheng.

Jess nodded. "I met her at the office. She's very beautiful."

Ah Cheng heard this in silence, then smiled mischievously. "In old days that one would have bound feet."

"I've heard about that," said Jess. "It made a woman's feet beautiful."

"Tiny feet sign of beauty," agreed Ah Cheng. "Also show wealth. Such a woman no work." She smiled again. "Bound feet keep woman at home, out of trouble. Husband no worry."

Jess was conscious of a great sadness. Of course a Chinese man could take more wives, concubines, even, do as he pleased, but the woman must observe other rules. The old double standard in action again. There seemed to be no stopping it.

"The old ways are best," said Ah Cheng solemnly. "Save much trouble."

Jess forgot herself and cried, "How can you say that? Those women were prisoners."

Ah Cheng considered. "Maybe so. But bound foot woman have very good life. No work in fields. Have rich clothes. Only need to please husband."

Jess was about to retort to this when she realized that Ah Cheng had a point. Such a life of luxury might look very good to a girl raised in extreme poverty.

"I don't know, Ah Cheng. I don't understand the relationship between men and women at all."

"Very simple," Ah Cheng replied, setting Jess's breakfast before her. "Men yang, women yin. Need both. World not work with only one."

"I suppose so," said Jess, picking up her fork. "I only wish I knew my place in things."

"That it!" cried Ah Cheng triumphantly. "Chinese woman know place. No ask questions. No worry. Everything told her. Easy."

Jess nodded and began her breakfast. In a certain sense Ah Cheng was right. It *was* easier to have things laid out for you, not to have to decide for yourself. If she had been married blind to Thorpe, for instance, she could have loved him without a struggle, considering it her duty. But, of course, it was bad for a person's growth to be kept in a childlike dependent state. And what of the poor women who were faced with husbands they couldn't even like, let alone love?

"Too bad you not have father find you husband," said Ah Cheng suddenly. "Time to put up your hair. You ready be woman."

To her confusion Jess blushed. "Sorry, Ah Cheng. Both my parents are gone. I guess if I want a husband, I'll have to find him myself."

"American way strange," said Ah Cheng. "I no like."

Jess made no further answer but contented herself with eating her breakfast. She certainly couldn't discuss her feelings for Thorpe with his housekeeper. And anyway, she wasn't really sure she knew what those feelings were. They ranged from a terrible intense longing to be in his arms to an equally intense desire to hit him with her fists. Surely such feelings could not be the basis of any reasonable adult relationship.

She finished off the breakfast and gave Ah Cheng a weak smile. "Thank you. I guess if we're leaving today I'd better be sure I have everything packed. Thank you for telling me about your life. I've learned a lot."

The little Chinese woman eyed her thoughtfully. "You need husband. Everything better then."

Jess managed a laugh but it was more out of nervousness than humor. "We've been talking too much about weddings, I'm afraid. You have such things on your mind. There's no husband in my future, none at all. Well, I'd better get busy. I want to be ready."

The morning flew as Jess checked everything and packed up. She was grateful that her khakis and boots showed the mark of wear. At least he could see she'd been in the wilderness before. She checked over the laces of her boots, all the buttons and zippers of pants and shirts. In the jungle replacements were impossible to find.

Once more she went over the list of accessories for the camera. She had filters, light meter, the flash attachment for dark recesses, everything she could think of.

With a sigh she packed everything into her backpack. It, too, showed signs of heavy wear. How many trips into the wilderness it had seen!

Everything that could be packed was ready and Jess set the pack by the door and wandered over to look out into the garden. It looked quite beautiful, but by now she knew better than to venture out in the heat of the day. Of course in the jungle it would be worse, damp and steamy and with insects everywhere.

Jess had a vivid memory picture of the cobra they had seen the day before. Such snakes lived all over in the jungle and from what she had heard they were quite easily angered. Well, she told herself, she would cross that bridge when she came to it. No use borrowing trouble.

She turned away from the window, plopped herself down on the bed. Her mind would not rest, mentally checking and rechecking her equipment. And then the picture of the cobra intervened again. The death's-head on its hood had been quite striking. Strange how nature gave such a warning.

In her memory Jess went back to her first experience with a snake. She could not remember her exact age, maybe two or three, maybe younger. But she had already become fascinated by animals. Every animal within reach had become her friend.

The memory was rather vague around the edges. She did not recall all the details. But she did remember quite vividly that the sun had been warm on her skin; evidently she had been playing in the yard by the ranch house and wandered a little distance away, engrossed by the antics of a favorite kitten chasing a butterfly.

Then she had spied the rattler, curled up on a rock enjoying the sun. And she had stopped to get to know him. She recalled no feeling of threat at first, only joy at this discovery of a new playmate. But when the snake reared its head, she drew back automatically. Nothing so ugly could be a friend, her child's mind had told her. And she turned and hurried back to the house, away from the creature that seemed so repulsive.

Jess sighed. She had had to learn as she was growing up that all creatures were not willing to be playmates, that some were quite dangerous. But she had learned and she had kept her love for animal life and for capturing it on film.

She turned on one side and cradled her head on her hand. She had no idea how many different kinds of animals she had filmed in those years since she'd had her first camera, but she had loved every minute of it.

Filming flowers would be different. They hadn't the personality of animals. There would be no action to save a picture in which the light wasn't quite right.

Jess sighed and shifted again in the bed. She was back to worrying about filters.

Fortunately at that moment the phone rang. Jess picked it up. "Hello?"

"This is Derek. I'm back from the city. Meet me in my office in five minutes, Jess."

As always the sound of her name on his lips did strange things to her. "All right, Derek."

A click told her that he had hung up and she replaced the receiver. Sharp and to the point, that was Derek Thorpe. No time for polite amenities. Just give orders. And have them obeyed, she thought bitterly.

She glanced quickly in the mirror and then shrugged. There was nothing to be done to improve her looks. Besides, he would soon see her in even worse condition. The jungle would not make her any more attractive.

Outside the office door she paused to take a deep breath. It was ridiculous to feel so in awe of him. He was only a man. Not some kind of god-figure. She had a sudden fantasy of him clothed in Greek garments, wearing a ferocious grin, and hurling thunderbolts from the clouds. He was just the sort to portray Zeus!

The thought made her smile and she pushed open the door. He looked up from the desk. "Good, Jess. You're prompt."

His face and his tone gave no sign that he remembered their altercation of the night before.

"Ah Cheng tells me we're leaving this afternoon," she said, striving to keep her voice even. If he meant to ignore what had happened, she would too.

Thorpe nodded. "I've ordered the plane to be made ready. I want you to check over these lists. Everything on them has been delivered to the plane. Make sure you haven't forgotten anything."

How neatly he had passed the responsibility on to her, she thought as she accepted the lists. She checked it carefully, double-checked it, in fact. But there was no doubt that it was complete.

"Everything is here," she said, conscious that his eyes were examining her carefully.

"Good. How have you outfitted yourself? This is rough terrain, you know."

"I know." Jess handed him back the lists and took a

chair. "I brought my usual wilderness gear, khakis and boots. My pack."

"What kind of boots?"

"They lace and they're waterproof," she replied. "I'm not a beginner. I've been on expeditions before."

"Into the rain forest?"

"No. But you act as though no other country is at all dangerous. America has some pretty rough wilderness areas, you know."

He shrugged. "Perhaps. But the rain forest *is* different. It has a different psychological effect on humans. You have to hack your way through such fecundity and you feel that the growth resumes as soon as you have passed. The rain forest teems with life— vegetable, animal, insect." He eyed her speculatively. "I suggest you wear your heaviest and tightest pants. You may scoff at the notion of leeches now. But once you've been bitten—and you will be—you'll find it no laughing matter."

"I am not laughing. I simply said I can handle it. I can handle anything a man can."

As she said this Jess thought ironically that a male photographer would be spared her worse problem. A man, at least, would not be drawn to Thorpe's magnetic maleness as she was.

"Well, I'll take your word on the clothes," he began.

"Thank you for believing that I have some sense," she retorted with sarcasm.

He raised a black eyebrow. "That still remains to be proved. Be ready at one and don't pack more than you can carry yourself. I'll have a bearer for the equipment later but your clothes are your concern."

Jess smiled stiffly. "Of course. I'm already packed and I assumed as much. I always carry my share."

He nodded and turned again to his papers.

So she was dismissed, thought Jess bitterly, dismissed

until he wanted her. And she rose and left the room, not exactly slamming the door behind her, but letting it close with enough force to cause the man at the desk to wince slightly.

She was ready and waiting in the foyer at five to one. It was good to be back in her old khakis and boots again. Some of her confidence came back to her.

Thorpe appeared exactly at one, wearing khakis and carrying a pack. He nodded when he saw her. "The equipment's already been loaded. Harrington will meet us at the airport. Are you sure you have everything?"

"Quite sure."

"Good. Then let's go."

The ride to the airport was made in silence, Thorpe leaning back in the seat with closed eyes. Jess, looking out the window at the teeming streets, tried to see if she could recognize anything from the day before. She was also intrigued by the variety of clothes worn by the passing women. The cheongsam seemed to be a favorite of many young Chinese women, perhaps because of its neat fit. Jess could not decide whether it or the sari was a lovelier way to dress. The Malayan sarong looked far too difficult to keep up, she thought. Then she smiled ruefully. What an odd occupation for the mind of a woman on her way into the rain forest.

Finally the car pulled up to the airport and Thorpe roused himself. "Well, here we are."

"We're flying out of Singapore International in a private plane?" said Jess.

Thorpe grinned. "We're not exactly flying a Piper Cub. My Learjet needs a little room. And besides, Singapore isn't all that big. All air traffic is controlled by the Air Traffic Control Centre. I have filed my flight plan already."

Shouldering her pack, Jess followed in a kind of daze as Thorpe made his way through the terminal to where

Harrington waited. All doors opened for him with ease and so Jess was not surprised to find that no one bothered to check her passport or her pack.

The plane itself made her pause. Learjet had meant nothing to her except that it included the word jet. But this was obviously a very expensive plane, very expensive.

As she followed the men aboard, she felt as though she were in a dream. The cabin was so richly appointed that it hardly looked like the cabin of a plane. She stowed her pack with the others and sank into a soft seat. Moments later Harrington settled beside her.

He spread a map across her knees. "I thought you might like to see where we're going," he said.

"I would. Thank you."

"Dick," said Thorpe, appearing suddenly. "Go up and ask the pilot if he checked the flight plan carefully."

Harrington gave his friend a pointed look, but rose and went forward.

Thorpe settled in the seat to Jess's right and touched the map. "Here is Malaya, on the left. Singapore is at the southern tip."

Jess remained silent. What was he up to now?

"Sarawak and Sabah are to the right. They're both part of Malaysia now. We'll fly east—this way across the China Sea to Kuching, Sarawak's capital. Then we'll take a land rover inland to visit the Land Dyaks. I have friends there."

He cast her a quizzical look and lowered his voice. "Speaking of *friends*," his tone gave the word a peculiar sound, *"you* certainly have made a hit with Harrington. That must have been quite a sightseeing trip."

Jess bit her lip to keep back the sharp words and contented herself with what she hoped was a disinterested shrug. Let him think whatever he liked, the conceited—

When she didn't answer, he returned his gaze to the map. "Then we'll drive back to Kuching and fly northeast to Sibu and go up the Rajang River to visit the Ibans or Sea Dyaks. Then back to Sibu and fly still further north to Tuaran. We're to meet Anggau, our guide, at Kota Belud, but we'll take a land rover there. Then it's off to Kinabalu."

Harrington returned and settled in the other seat. "He says everything is fine."

Thorpe nodded. "We'd better fasten our seat belts," he said rather sharply. He could be almost uncivil, Jess thought irritably, as her fingers fumbled with the catch. Then they were airbound, but the men flanking her, though they occasionally exchanged hard glances, remained silent and finally Jess dozed. If she knew Thorpe, she would need every ounce of her strength to get through the days ahead.

She was roused by Harrington. "Time to wake up, Jess. We've reached Kuching."

Jess nodded and pulled herself erect in the seat.

It appeared that Thorpe was just as well known at the Kuching Airport as in Singapore for he was greeted with smiles all around and a land rover was waiting, complete with a brown-skinned, grinning driver. Thorpe dismissed the man and took the driver's seat himself.

As Jess settled in the back seat, she wondered if Thorpe ever went anyplace where he was treated like an ordinary person. Somehow she doubted it.

As the land rover left the city and bumped along into the interior, Jess watched with interest.

"There used to be many wayside shrines," said Harrington. "The people put offerings there at rice planting time to appease evil spirits. We'll see some when we're walking."

Out the window Jess saw attempts to tame the jungle. Swamps were planted with long rows of palms. "Sago," said Harrington. "It's used primarily for food, though in other places they stiffen textiles with it."

Later they passed burned-off hillsides that had been planted. Jess turned to Harrington again. "Tapioca," he grinned. "Also for eating."

Jess grinned back. "That, I've eaten."

"The government's been after the natives," interrupted Thorpe, "trying to get them to use irrigation instead of burning off new land every year. The waste in the old way is frightful. The land has to lie fallow for a long time to regain its fertility."

Jess frowned, "I suppose people think the old ways are best."

Finally the car bumped to a halt. "Time to walk," said Thorpe with obvious satisfaction. "Bring your pack. We'll spend the night in the longhouse."

"It's a good thing you brought plenty of film," said Harrington. "You'll want to get some shots of these people."

Jess shouldered her pack and looked at the jungle around her. It seemed very dense and green. Then Thorpe started out and she had no more time for looking. The track wound, climbed, dipped. She followed Thorpe across narrow bamboo bridges that swayed nerve-wrackingly over deep ravines and down paths where the jungle seemed determined to grow back across the narrow way. Wherever he led, she followed and always without a word or a murmur of exhaustion. In fact, now that they were finally moving Jess felt a certain exhilaration. Now she would be able to show him.

Finally Thorpe stopped. Beside the trail stood a rough-hewn wooden bench and on it sat a pipe.

Harrington smiled. "The bench and the pipe are for the use of weary travelers. Or spirits who happen to be passing this way," he explained.

"Evil spirits or good ones?" asked Jess curiously.

"It doesn't really matter. Both must be propitiated."

"If this instant lesson in native religion is finished," said Thorpe curtly, "perhaps we can move on. Unless you want to rest."

The latter was directed to Jess and, even if she had been dropping from exhaustion, she would have refused the offer. "No, I'm fine."

"Then let's move."

They walked for some time longer, Jess blessing the sturdy body that enabled her to keep pace with the men. And then they reached the summit of a small hill and she caught her breath. Beneath them wound a river and stretched out beside it, separated only by a thin line of cultivated palms, was a longhouse. It was built on stilts and terraced and it stretched up one hill as far as she could see then dipped and disappeared into the jungle.

"It's so big," she breathed.

"Last year more than seventy families lived here."

Jess shook her head. That was a lot of togetherness.

As they drew nearer, she saw pigs and chickens foraging in the cleared spaces under the house. Several dogs came up to sniff at her suspiciously. Above on the veranda were men mending fish nets and women pounding rice.

They approached the notched log that led up to the longhouse. "The Dyaks were headhunters," said Thorpe. "They built their villages on stilts for protection. The log ladder was drawn up after them."

Jess nodded. So it was headhunters now. If he hoped to frighten her with that, he was mistaken. She scrambled nimbly up the ladder after him and was instantly surrounded by smiling girls. Whatever these people had once been they seemed very friendly now.

She was momentarily startled by someone waving a squawking chicken over their heads. But she soon figured it must have some ritual significance. Then young girls advanced with cups of liquid. She watched Thorpe closely and saw that he took only a sip from each cup before returning it to the giver. She did likewise.

The liquid was warm, of course, and must have been some kind of beer. Jess thanked the etiquette that allowed her to forego drinking large quantities of it.

Then she followed as Thorpe and Harrington first shed their packs and then moved into an inner room. It was cool and clean there and she was glad to follow their example and sit cross-legged on the floor mats. Soon more girls brought out plates of rice, eggs, tobacco, betel nuts, and salt. They set the plates before Thorpe in rows of seven. Solemnly he took something from each plate and put it on a larger one. Then he was offered chicken feathers dipped in blood.

Jess held her breath as he lightly touched her with the feathers, repeated the act for those near him, and then put them on top of the food.

The man who had waved the chicken waved it again. Thorpe did the same. Then someone took it away.

Beside her Harrington whispered. "That dish will be put aside for the spirits. We'll eat the rest. Some longhouses have forsaken many of the old ways. But this chief is very conservative. He believes in the old customs and keeps them alive."

Jess partook of the food on the plates, though

sparingly. And later, while Thorpe was in serious discussion with the chief, she rose to wander about the longhouse with Harrington.

Along the wide veranda people were busy at work. One boy was weaving a casting net, another was making a cane paddle. Some people were scraping the pith from logs.

"Sago," explained Harrington. "They stomp it into a pulp and save it. They'll use it for hard times when the rice isn't good."

An old woman was weaving a blanket. Jess stopped to admire it. The pattern was quite lovely, showing hornbills calling from the top of a durian tree. All around was a feeling of peace. Jess sighed. Perhaps this was something of what Ah Cheng meant by 'family.'

Harrington smiled at her. "Life here is very different. Behind the plank wall, in rooms like the one we were in, each family has its own sleeping quarters. And on this veranda side a work space. But this is a real communal life. They work together and share."

As he spoke several smiling women came up the ladder carrying baskets of vegetables. Then there was the sound of barking and Harrington grinned. "A couple of village dogs must be having a disagreement."

Jess smiled. "I like this place. It has a good feeling."

"Harrington!" Thorpe's voice came to them through the pleasant noises.

"Coming."

Jess followed to where Thorpe still sat with the chief, only now on the wide veranda.

"Our host has consented to show us a war dance." Thorpe turned cold eyes on Jess. "The kind they did in the old days in preparation for going after heads."

Jess regarded him evenly. If he expected to scare her that easily, he was mistaken. "That should be interesting," she said as she settled cross-legged on the woven mat beside him.

She looked carefully at the chief's outfit. He wore a sarong of a bright plaid design, not very jungle-looking. But around his neck hung some sort of shaggy animal skin, ornamented in front with a great pearly shell.

Jess leaned toward Harrington. "Is that an animal skin he's wearing?"

Dick nodded. "It's his war coat. Made of goatskin."

As the chief rose and moved toward the center of the floor, Jess saw that the back of his war coat was decorated with long hornbill feathers. He also wore a war bonnet that looked like it was made on a bamboo frame. Barred hornbill feathers decorated the front and trailed out behind.

The chief consulted with one of the men who rose immediately and went into the longhouse. In a moment he returned, carrying a curious-looking stringed instrument. Thorpe leaned toward her. "That's a *sape*, rather like a guitar."

As the first sounds issued from the *sape* the people began to gather. They crowded around the mat where the chief stood, but they were careful not to obstruct the view of their guests.

On the other side of Thorpe a short scarred man squatted. "He'll interpret the movements," said Thorpe. "I will repeat it in English."

And then the dance began. There was a certain insistence to the beat that Jess found disturbing. As the chief stomped and swayed, his bare feet pounding the mat, the soft guttural tones of the interpreter had a hypnotic quality to them.

Thorpe's deep voice moved against it like dark clouds against a pale sky. "The men go out," he said. "They hunt for the enemy. They peer through the jungle. We must take the enemy's head. We are strong. We will win. We will not allow the enemy to take our heads. When we have their heads, we will be very strong."

Jess suppressed a shudder. She would not let Thorpe see that this disturbed her.

"We hang the enemy heads in our rafters. We keep their spirits as our slaves," Thorpe continued, his rich, deep tones giving the words added import.

Jess fought the sudden urge to look up. Were there human skulls hanging in the shadows above her?

"We are strong," repeated Thorpe. "We will win. We are mighty men. We will bring home many heads."

Finally the chief's dance was over. Jess smiled and nodded her appreciation with the rest, but she felt uneasy. These shy and gentle people had once hunted heads! It seemed unreal.

She turned to Thorpe. "I never do portrait shots, but I would like to take a few pictures here. Will you see if the chief minds?"

There were some moments of talk and then Thorpe returned. "The chief says it's fine. I suggest you start with him. Only he wants to get something first, he said, something to show you."

Jess nodded. "I'll just get my camera."

The packs were only a short distance away and as she took out her equipment she thought with a smile that she would have to get some shots of Ah Cheng when she returned. This trip was bringing out new facets of her career that had not previously interested her.

Then she moved back to where Harrington and Thorpe still sat. The chief had returned and was holding something in his hand. He advanced proudly toward her and struck a warlike pose, one outstretched hand holding a net bag full of—Jess's stomach lurched violently. Dear God, she wouldn't have to look in the rafters. The chief's net bag was full of human skulls!

She swallowed several times and then, aware that Thorpe was watching her closely, she forced a smile onto her lips and moved closer to the chief. "Will you ask him to stand over there?" she said calmly to Thorpe.

He nodded. Soon the chief was posed by the edge of the veranda, the dense green of the jungle making a dramatic backdrop.

She took several shots, with the grisly trophies in full view.

"Please thank the chief," she said finally. "And ask if I can take some pictures of the longhouse and of his people working."

"He's already said you can. I have promised to bring him a picture next time. He'll be pleased to see his trophies on film. I also told him that many men would know of his prowess as a warrior."

"I see." Jess refused to meet Thorpe's eyes. She had the feeling he was waiting, always waiting, for her to fail. And then he meant to gloat and say, 'I told you so.' But she would not give him that satisfaction, she told herself firmly as she moved away to get some shots of the people in their natural state.

Some time later she returned, put her equipment away again, and settled back beside Harrington, where she thought with longing of that sunken tub in Singapore.

"Tired?" he asked.

Jess shook her head. "No, this is very interesting."

Harrington nodded and smiled at her. "Remember when I told you about birds' nest soup?"

Jess nodded.

"Well, Derek has refreshed my memory. There are

nest factories right on Sarawak, further up the coast at Niah."

"It sounds unbelievable."

"It isn't. There are limestone hills honeycombed with immense caves. Bats and swiftlets both inhabit them. But it's the swiftlets' nests that they use. The nest collectors go in with torches. The birds build their nests on the cave ceilings, using a salivary excretion. The collectors are quite daring, actually. They have to be to use the rickety concoctions of bamboo, rattan, and wood that they clamber up to reach the highest nests."

Jess wrinkled her nose. "Their effort is wasted on me, I'm afraid."

Harrington grinned. "You haven't yet achieved gourmet tastes."

Jess returned his grin. "You're right. And I don't think I ever will."

They were still grinning at each other when Thorpe approached with several lengths of colorful material over his arm. "Bath time," he said with a curious smile.

"Bath?" Jess was surprised.

"On the other side of the longhouse is the river. We go to bathe together. This is your sarong."

He dropped one piece of material into her lap.

"I don't know how to wear a sarong," Jess cried, aware of rising panic in her voice.

Thorpe shrugged. "If you want a bath today, you'd better learn in a hurry. Leave your other clothes here." And he turned away.

Jess was tired and sweaty and she longed for the cool water of the river, but the idea of the sarong was ridiculous.

Harrington smiled gently. "It's really not so difficult," he said. "You take off your boots and socks first. Then undress under the sarong."

Jess eyed him incredulously. "And what holds it up while I'm undressing?"

"Watch." Harrington stripped off boots and socks, shed his shirt, wrapped the sarong neatly around his waist, and stepped out of his trousers. "See, it's easy."

Jess could not help laughing, though she was aware that much of it was nervous laughter. "I think you've forgotten something," she said. "Things are somewhat more complicated for a woman."

"Come on, Jess," prompted Harrington softly. "You said you could handle anything a man can."

He was right, Jess thought as she tugged at boots and socks. She *had* said that. And she would probably regret it many times before this expedition was over.

By using the sarong like a cape she managed to get out of her shirt and bra. Then, by a certain amount of judicious maneuvering she got the material around her in sarong fashion, but she was at a loss as to how to continue.

"You're doing great, Jess. Don't quit now," said Harrington.

"But—but I don't know how to fasten it."

Harrington grinned mischievously. "You wrap it around and tuck it in. Like this." And he demonstrated swiftly.

Jess swallowed several times as she nervously tried to duplicate his movements. Oh what she wouldn't have given for a good old American safety pin! One wrong move and she would be left naked. The thought frightened her so that for a moment she couldn't continue.

Harrington seemed to take pity on her. "Do you want me to stand behind you and hold the top while you loosen your trousers?"

"Yes, Dick, thank you."

With his help Jess managed to loosen her trousers and step out of them and her underwear. With one hand on the top of her sarong, she hurriedly bundled her clothing up. It was obvious that these women knew nothing of brassieres and panties. And she did not want to enlighten them. Not with Derek Thorpe standing by!

Until this moment she had not thought much about the half-nude state of some of the older women. They were obviously at home that way so that there was nothing embarrassing about it. But now, even in her sarong, she felt naked—and vulnerable.

As she turned she found Thorpe's eyes on her and she flushed scarlet, her hand going automatically to the top of her sarong.

And then she saw *him*. While she had been busy maneuvering under the sarong, he had divested himself of his Western garb. In the shadows of the veranda he looked almost like a native himself, except that these people were thin and slightly built and Derek Thorpe's bare bronzed chest was wide and powerful, and covered with a thick mat of curly black hair.

Even from a distance she could see the glint in his eye as he surveyed her. Again she clutched automatically at the top of her sarong.

He gave her a sardonic grin and stepped closer. "You make quite a different kind of native," he said, his eyes going to her red hair. "The chief has offered me a large price for you. He said it would give him considerable prestige to have a red-haired woman."

Jess gasped. "You're—you're out of line, Mr. Thorpe. Such things are no longer allowed." She knew he meant to bait her, to get a rise out of her, but Jess couldn't help feeling indignant.

His eyes shifted from her hair to the rapid rise and fall of her breasts under the sarong and it was only with the greatest effort that she forced herself not to clutch spasmodically at the material.

"Your sense of humor is deserting you already," he said with that terrible smile that melted her bones. "And we haven't really seen the jungle yet. Actually the chief did ask me where I got you. He has a yen for a new woman. But I told him you were taken—that you were mine."

For a long moment he looked into her eyes and Jess felt her knees begin to tremble. She wanted to tell him that he had been wrong, that he had no right to say such things, but somehow the words wouldn't come. And deep within her surged the bitter realization that she wished his words *were* true. Some primeval part of herself, some part quite beyond the reach of sense or reason, wanted most desperately to surrender to the powerful male force in him.

His eyes slid over her in a tantalizing way and he smiled again. "I'm afraid there's a small price to be paid for my defense of your honor."

Still Jess could not answer.

"We will have to bathe together. The chief expects it. Come." And he took her trembling hand in his and led her toward the log ladder.

For a second at the top of the ladder Jess balked. How could she negotiate that slippery ladder clothed in this single piece of cloth that might drop off at any moment?

"Shall I carry you down?" asked Thorpe with a glint in his eye.

For one wild moment she was about to say yes and then she shook her head. "Of course not. You go first."

He smiled at her mockingly. "Anything you say, kitten. Just be careful of your sarong." And he moved lightly down the slippery ladder with that grace that so reminded her of a great cat.

Jess took a deep breath. The best way would be to go fast. She would look really ridiculous teetering about on each step. And, fortunately, the sarong was not long enough to tangle around her ankles. She had a brief picture of herself lying naked in the dirt at the bottom of the ladder and then, gathering up her courage, she hurried after Thorpe.

The log was wet and slippery under her bare feet; she felt her toes curling under to grip the wood. And then she was down. Breathless and a little giddy, but down—and with the sarong still in place.

"You did that like a veteran," said Harrington as he joined them a moment later.

"Thank you." Jess felt strangely lightheaded as Thorpe took her hand in his again and moved off. She knew that she should withdraw her hand, but she did not try to. She felt somehow that she had become a part of this jungle community. What happened here had very little to do with the world out there. Here there were only men and women—and the force that pulled them so powerfully together.

As they approached the river, Jess saw that the shallows were already crowded with people and many of the younger women had dropped their sarongs to their waists.

"Relax," said Thorpe in that mocking tone she had grown so to dislike. "You don't have to follow their example. We just wade in and splash around. Let the river wash away the grime."

"No soap," added Harrington from behind her. "Nothing to pollute the environment."

Jess turned to give him a smile and then Thorpe was pulling her into the stream.

There was not much current and yet the first slight tug at the hem of her sarong caused Jess to start with alarm. But Thorpe kept wading out and, since he still had her hand, she was forced to follow him.

The water felt wonderful, but she grew increasingly aware of the changing texture of the river bed beneath her bare toes. This was, after all, a jungle river, inhabited by jungle wildlife. What kind of life lurked unseen beneath her feet?

But her attention was soon wrested from that thought as Thorpe reached water about knee-high and suddenly sat down, pulling her off-balance, into the water beside him. The water caught at the top of the sarong and she felt it begin to give. She grabbed at it frantically with one hand as she floundered to an upright position beside him.

"Come, Jess," said Thorpe. "You must learn to be more confident. You can't always go about grasping your clothes."

He was frankly laughing at her and for one wild moment she considered releasing her hold on the now loosened sarong. Then sanity returned.

"I suggest, Mr. Thorpe, that your anatomy is somewhat better designed for wearing such things."

Harrington, settling into the water on her other side, chuckled, but Thorpe did not smile.

"Nonsense, Jess," Thorpe said briskly. "Your anatomy is quite sufficient to the task. And a lovely anatomy it is, too. Here, you must simply learn to do it right. Then you can walk about in perfect safety and comfort."

And while she watched paralyzed, he removed the material from her hand and tucked it expertly in. In the process his hands grazed the top of her half-exposed breast and Jess felt as though he had left the print of his fingers there. All sorts of sharp, stinging retorts came to her mind, but none of them got to her lips.

"That should convince the chief, eh Harrington?" said Thorpe.

"If he needs convincing," said Harrington dryly. "I suppose it would."

Suddenly Jess grew conscious of the coolness of the water. It felt so good on her skin which was warm and dirty after their trek through the jungle. There was something familiar about the feel of it, thought Jess vaguely, but it wasn't like the sweet-scented water of the sunken tub. No, it was— Yes, that was it. It was more like the feel of the silken sheets in her room. The cool water seemed to caress her skin just as the silk did. It was a strangely intimate feeling. Would a man's hands— She stopped short at the thought, flushing scarlet.

"There's nothing to be embarrassed about here," said Harrington. "Everything is very natural. Close to the land." He looked around. "Dyaks always build their longhouses near a river. Now, of course, some of them send their children away to school. Sometimes that ruins them for life here. And they begin to long for the trappings of civilization, expecially guns and boat motors."

"There's a great deal of sense to their longings," said Thorpe. "A tribe of hunters *should* value guns—they make the arduous job of getting food easier. And so may the motor for a fishing people."

"You're right, of course," admitted Harrington. "Still, there are other things—like the transistor radios they're so fond of. They don't seem very helpful."

"I could say that they give weather information," said Thorpe, "but that would be begging the question. The Dyaks, like others, are curious. And the possession of certain things, in any culture, marks one as above average. In our society we value great cars and houses. The Dyak's most prized possession, however, is usually his collection of heads."

Unconsciously Jess grimaced.

"They were forbidden to hunt heads by the government," Thorpe continued. "But during World War II the ban was lifted against the Japanese who tried to hide out in the jungle. It may seem bad to us, but of course the Dyaks don't see it that way."

Jess shivered.

"Certainly you're aware by now, Jess, that these are not a cruel people. Their culture differs, that's all. Instead of medals a man displays his enemies' heads. Very sensible. Besides, in spite of the ferocity of the dance, the Land Dyaks were very gentle people. They took heads only in self-defense and moved inland expressly to escape the more ferocious Sea Dyaks."

He looked at Jess. "Tomorrow we'll fly to Sibu and then ride up the Rajang River. You can see some Sea Dyaks, or Ibans as they're called. In the old days they were the famous 'wild men of Borneo.' Ferociously tattooed, they preyed on everyone in sight, pirating up and down the coast and terrorizing. Sometimes they took heads and sometimes they sold the captured Land Dyaks as slaves to the rich merchants at Brunei."

Jess shivered again. It seemed that people had always been intent on enslaving each other. But there were other kinds of slavery, she thought as Thorpe's bare arm brushed hers, other kinds of slavery far more degrading than that imposed on a captive by his conqueror. For instance, there was this insane longing within her to submit, no—surrender was the better word—to yield herself completely to him.

As she looked around her at the happy, smiling people, she thought how fortunate they all were. Even the encroachments of civilization had not yet forced them to question their roles. They *knew* how they were to behave, what their limits were. A woman did not have to compete with men. In fact, such a thing was unthinkable. She sighed. Thorpe had been right about one thing. Life in the jungle was clearer, less complicated. If only they could leave civilization behind them.

But what, said the sane sensible part of herself, what would happen when their passion was sated, as passion so soon was? Clearly she would not be happy gathering vegetables and pounding sago the rest of her life. No, without her camera she was incomplete, not a whole person.

Thorpe stood up. "Time to go back for dinner."

Jess hesitated, only now realizing that a wet sarong would be even more revealing than a dry one. But she could not remain sitting in the river all night. That, at least, was clear.

With a sigh she took his outstretched hand. She was fearful for the sarong, but though the water made it heavy and it clung to her in a way that made her want to drop into the water again, it remained securely tucked.

"The sarong," said Thorpe with that wicked mocking smile, "was certainly one of man's most marvelous inventions." And he carefully inspected her.

Jess, striving to remain indifferent under the speculative gaze of those gray eyes, fastened her own eyes on his bare chest. Little droplets of water glistened in the hair there. She found to her distress that she wanted to reach out and touch him. Even worse, she wanted to throw herself against that chest!

"If you've seen enough," she said pointedly. "Perhaps we should follow the others."

"I haven't seen nearly enough," he replied. "But I suppose it's unlikely that I'll see anymore, so we might as well go back."

What gall the man had, thought Jess, halfway between anger and admiration. He was so blatant about whatever he wanted and he probably usually got it. But not this time, she told herself firmly, not this time.

By the time they reached the longhouse the sarong had begun to dry. But the men did not resume their clothes and Jess determined to do as they did.

The evening meal was soon served—rice and some sort of meat cut in little pieces. Jess ate sparingly of the meat, not knowing its origin. Its flavor she found rather different and she was about to ask Harrington when she thought better of it. If she were eating something unusual, it was probably better not to know it.

And then from his place beside her Thorpe passed the meat again. "Have some more monkey," he said conversationally.

The contents of Jess's stomach fought violently to escape and she thought fleetingly that it would serve him right if she got sick all over him. But she did not. She smiled once and said politely, "No thank you. I've had enough for tonight."

After that, of course, she could hardly take any more rice, but it really didn't matter. She had lost all her appetite. She supposed Thorpe felt justified in treating her as he did. After all, she had continually insisted that she could handle anything a man could.

But this was not easy. Her mind kept presenting her with pictures of monkeys and her stomach surged in constant revolt. Finally, when she judged that enough time had passed so that Thorpe would not make any connections she rose and moved toward the ladder. They would think she was going to relieve the call of nature.

But as soon as Jess reached the privacy of the jungle's

edge, she lost her supper. Her knees were weak and shaky and her throat felt on fire, but at least her stomach no longer surged and rioted with its unwelcome burden.

She brushed back her hair and scrubbed at her mouth. Then, a little unsteadily, she made her way back to the veranda.

The log ladder seemed easier to negotiate with every use and even unsteady as she was she reached the top successfully.

As she resumed her seat, Thorpe, with wicked humor in his eyes, leaned closer to ask, "Are you all right?"

"Fine," lied Jess stoutly. She would die before she admitted anything to him.

When dusk fell, everyone went inside the longhouse and settled down. Jess was a little disturbed to find that Thorpe shared the same sleeping room. But then she discovered that Harrington would be using it, too, and she felt slightly more at ease.

It took her some time to fall off to sleep. The sounds of so many people around her, of the animals under the house, of the jungle that was so near, were different and intriguing, but it was the sound of Thorpe's even breathing from the pallet so close to her own and the memory of him clad in that sarong, so primitive, so powerful, so male, that kept her from getting the sleep she needed.

The sound of singing birds woke her at first light and, clutching her sarong, she crept from the room. She would go to the river early and be back in her regular clothes before anyone else was up. She did not believe that she could stand to have Thorpe bathe beside her again—so close and yet so far away.

As she crept carefully out of the room and onto the veranda, the sounds of the jungle grew more pronounced. It was almost like she could *hear* things growing.

The boards of the veranda felt cool under her bare feet and a fresh clean smell came to her from the jungle.

She made her way easily down the notched log ladder. It was really a simple matter with no skeptical gray eyes fastened upon her, she thought ruefully. Of course, if one were born and raised in the longhouse, using the ladder would be almost second nature.

As she reached the packed dirt at the bottom a sleepy dog raised its head and surveyed her curiously. Then, apparently satisfied that she belonged, it put its head back on its paws and closed its eyes.

Jess moved softly along the hard-packed trail. Fortunately the bare feet of more than seventy families kept the vegetation off the path. She would not step unaware on some insect life.

She passed the small stand of cultivated palms and stood looking at the river. The water, now undisturbed by any bodies, was limpid and clear. It was quite wide and shallow at this point, probably the reason the village had been established here in the first place, she thought.

From the jungle on the other side of the river came the songs of several birds. How fertile the rain forest was, thought Jess, impressed by the intense greenness of the foliage around her. Montana's plains with their buffalo grass and sagebrush, had nothing to equal this green. And even the wildernesses where she had worked had not been so lush, with greenness everywhere. It was certainly a good thing she had the green filter, she thought.

For a long hesitant moment Jess stood, unwilling to disturb the river's placid flow. And then, realizing that the others would be waking before too long, she stepped into the water. It was cool and refreshing and she was reminded again of the silken sheets in the Singapore room.

She waded further out. Perhaps she should just splash her face and arms. Then, unexplainably, she felt an urge to have the water on her bare skin. Slowly she eased the material up around her hips as she settled into the water. A convenient branch hanging out over the stream would make a good hook for the sarong, she thought, and as the water closed around her waist she reached up and hung the material there.

Jess settled naked into the water with a great sigh. The feeling was very different than it had been with the wet sarong clinging to her. All her senses seemed to be concentrated on the surface of her skin.

And then she heard a sound behind her. Her first impulse was to reach for the sarong, but that would bring her up out of the water. Instead she moved deeper under and turned.

Derek Thorpe stood on the shore. That same mysterious smile crossed his face. "You were serious about those baths, weren't you, Jess?" he said in that deep voice that made her quiver. "I am, too. Think I'll join you." And his hands went to the sarong at his waist.

"No!" Jess heard the panic in her voice. "That is—I'm coming out."

His eyes gleamed at her. "Fine. I'll wait." And he stood patiently, his eyes intent on her flushed face.

Dear God, thought Jess, was he going to stand there and watch till she stood up? She tried to figure out how she could maneuver so as to have her back to him, at least. But now she was sitting on the bottom and the branch with the sarong was between her and the shore where he stood.

"Here, I'll help you," he said and with a grin that

showed how much he relished her predicament, he strode into the water.

Desperately Jess sought to cover herself with her hands. The water was so clear that up close it concealed very little. He came to a stop directly in front of her and took the sarong from the limb.

"Here. I'll hold it."

"I'll hold it myself," said Jess, reaching up for it. But he held it just out of her reach.

"Stand up, Jess. You don't want to get your sarong all wet again. Stand up and I'll put it around you."

She longed for something sharp and bitter to say to him, but no words would come. And, to make matters worse, that wild part of her urged her to stand, to reveal herself to him.

"Come on, Jess," he said, still wearing that terrible smile. "I can't wait around here all day. We have to get back to Kuching."

"Please," she begged, "just give it to me and leave."

He shook his head. "I can't leave you alone in the river. A crocodile might get you."

"Derek!"

He waited a moment longer and then shrugged and turned toward the shore, the sarong slung over his arm. "Suit yourself. You can wait till the tribe comes out. Maybe the chief will help you."

"Derek! Come back!"

He turned and grinned at her. "Then you have to get out of the water like a good girl. All right?"

Jess nodded. There seemed nothing else to do.

He stood there holding the sarong, that wicked look in his eyes, and she took a deep breath and slowly rose from the water. She saw his eyes move over her nakedness and she felt the blood rushing to her cheeks. Then, very slowly, he wrapped her in the sarong and tucked it neatly in. Her flesh quivered where he had touched her and she fought an insane urge to throw herself against his bare chest.

"You've nothing to be ashamed of, Jess. Nothing at all. You're a very beautiful woman."

That wild thing inside her made her raise her eyes to his then and ask, "Oh, have I become a woman now?"

He smiled and shook his head. "Not quite, Jess. Not quite. But you're getting there."

And then he took her in his arms. She tried to stop him, to struggle, but she had to fight not only him but her own desires.

His hand on her bare back sent tremors through her flesh. His new beard seemed strange against her skin as his mouth moved, tenderly, persuasively, on hers. Here was no brutality, but a gentle, patient persuasion. The wild thing inside Jess surged again. The thin sarongs that separated them seemed to vanish and she felt her body melting into his as his lips teased hers, gently, tenderly, forcing them open until his tongue invaded her mouth. Jess whimpered and clung to him.

When finally he released her mouth, his lips moved softly along the curve of her throat and over her shoulder to the firm roundness of her breast where the top of the sarong ended.

Jess felt faint. She could not resist him; she knew that now. The powerful male force in him evoked some primitive female response in her, a response that no amount of reasoning could subdue. And so she was silent as his hands moved toward the place where the sarong was tucked in. She had no will to resist him. None at all.

Then suddenly from the shore came the sound of someone clearing his throat. "I hate to disturb you," Harrington said dryly. "But the longhouse is waking and the people will soon be here."

"Of course, thank you, Dick." Thorpe spoke as

nonchalantly as if he had just been given the weather for the day. His fingers moved over the tuck of her sarong. "All is secure, Jess. You're far too nervous about such things. No need to worry about this one. When I wrap a sarong, it stays wrapped."

As Thorpe led her from the water, Jess avoided Harrington's eyes. It was hard to say how much he had seen, evidently it had been more than enough. But as she followed Thorpe back to the longhouse, the uppermost thought in her mind was the question: what would have happened if Harrington hadn't come along when he did?

To her dismay Jess was sure she knew the answer. Whether it was infatuation or love no longer mattered. If Derek Thorpe had chosen to take her at that moment, she knew with sinking certainty that she would have let him. She would have surrendered to him there in the river—and done it gladly!

# Chapter 5

Jess remembered little of their goodbyes or the trek back to the land rover. She followed wherever Thorpe led and, when they reached the land rover, she settled into the seat silently.

Fortunately, Thorpe was too busy driving to pay attention to her and Jess closed her eyes and pretended to be resting. But, though her body was still, her mind was in turmoil.

When they reached Kuching, she could tell Thorpe she had changed her mind and didn't want to continue. He would take her back to Singapore, she was sure of that. And he would laugh all the way because he had proved her wrong!

*She* knew that it was not the jungle but Thorpe himself that terrified her. But she could not tell *him* that. He would probably laugh even harder at such information.

She was still unsure what to do when they reached Kuching. But at the airport, when Thorpe gave the car keys back to the driver and turned to her to say, "Well, kitten, ready for the *real* jungle?" she knew she had no choice.

She could not run, not with his laughter echoing behind her. She merely shrugged and replied, "As ready as you are."

And so the Learjet took to the air again and was soon setting down at Sibu. "We should reach the Sea Dyak settlement before dark," said Thorpe, consulting his watch. "If they have the boat ready."

Very soon they had negotiated the traffic of the town and Thorpe was helping her into the speedboat.

"This is the Rajang River," said Harrington, settling beside her. "It runs east and west across the country. The Sea Dyaks live along its banks. It's navigable far inland and they used to come down in their boats and take to the sea to pirate."

"How do they live now?" asked Jess. "Since pirating of that kind is forbidden."

"They raise crops: rubber, pepper, sago, coconuts, and rice. And they fish. And remember the glories of the old days. Undoubtedly the men will bring out their heads to show you. Actually, like all the tribes, they were ordered to give the heads Christian burial. That was before World War II when the government began to frown upon such things. But some men just hid theirs. After all, there's an identity thing here.

"Anyway, the men of this longhouse know and trust Derek. And like all of us they like to boast about their prowess."

"What about the women?" asked Jess.

"They work the gardens and care for the children. Time-honored female tasks," interrupted Thorpe curtly.

Jess had no reply for this. There was little point in defending women's rights to a man like Thorpe. It was like—Jess smiled grimly—like taking pictures with an empty camera!

As the speedboat made its way up the river Jess tried to relax. She was tired because she had not slept well. Perhaps if she shut her eyes she could imagine herself back in civilization, away from the jungle, and from Thorpe.

She must have dozed off, for suddenly Harrington was waking her. "We've arrived, Jess."

She sat up and rubbed her eyes. Several natives were pulling the speedboat up onto the shore. Before her stood another longhouse, built parallel to the river so that one could almost step from the log ladder directly into the river.

Further along batches of children splashed and played in the water. Little babies, supported by their mothers, gurgled happily as they paddled.

"The Ibans love water," said Harrington softly. "They always build as close to it as possible. They're skilled boatmen and powerful swimmers. In the old days, so they say, they settled disputes by water. The man who stayed under longer won."

Jess looked at him in surprise, but his face remained serious. "It's true, Jess. Also, the Ibans especially prize motors. Few of their boats are paddled now."

Thorpe gave her a sidelong glance. "The really modern Iban sometimes measures his standing by the horsepower of his *prau's* outboard rather than his count of heads."

"What sort of weapons did they use?" asked Jess, fascinated in spite of herself by the logistics of the thing.

"They used a *parang,*" said Thorpe. "A big sharp knife, handy for hacking through jungle. Of course when they could get firearms they used them, too. But the *parang* was particularly useful for removing heads."

Jess, intent on the life around her, made no reply. The boat had been beached and, as she climbed out, she saw immediately that these were a stronger, hardier people than the Land Dyaks. Every grown man sported elaborate tattoos and some had long, distended earlobes.

"Men and women used to wear heavy weights in their ears," explained Harrington at her look.

They were greeted ceremoniously and urged up to the veranda where they were offered the traditional refreshments. Then, as Thorpe seemed about to settle down with several men, she asked, "Will it be all right for me to take some shots here, too?"

Thorpe spoke with one of the men and then nodded. "The *penghulu,* the chief, says it's okay."

"Good." Jess unslung her case and dug out the camera. First she wanted to have a picture of the mothers and babies splashing in the river. Somewhere in the back of her mind, a photo story was forming. She was not sure as yet what focus it would take, but it would have something to do with male-female roles and the relative simplicity of living in the jungle.

"Mind if I tag along?" asked Harrington.

"Of course not," said Jess. "It's always good to have a friend."

"Speaking of friends," said Harrington as they reached the bottom of the log ladder, "I hope you aren't upset with me."

"Whatever for?" asked Jess in surprise.

"Well, I did sort of intrude on you at the river. I'm sorry. I didn't mean to."

"No, no," replied Jess quickly. "I'm glad you came." That was only half a lie, she thought.

Harrington frowned. "It didn't look to me like you were anxious for help."

Jess didn't know what to say to this and kept silent.

"I know it's none of my business," he went on. "But Derek's not for you. He lives in a different world. Have you forgotten Haviland—and Helen Cheong?"

"Of course not," Jess replied tartly. "I'm not about to become a member of Derek's little harem."

Harrington's face lightened a little. "I'm glad to hear

that. I really am. But he's not an easy man to deal with. And he usually gets what he wants."

"I know that," Jess said with a hint of bitterness. "But I'll manage."

Harrington frowned again. "I don't know why he's been so rough on you. Like last night—about the monkey meat."

Jess gave an involuntary spasm of revulsion.

"That wasn't really monkey," he said. "It was the chicken the chief had been waving about earlier."

"But it tasted different!" How like Thorpe, she thought. To make her as uncomfortable as possible!

"It was cooked in a different sauce. The natives do eat monkeys—certain edible species. They used to hunt them with poisoned darts and a blowgun. Often times the blowgun was taller than the man."

Jess moved away from the railing and they continued to walk, stopping now and then while she took a shot of a woman weaving or a man mending nets.

Once they came upon a group of boys solemnly sitting in a circle, intent on one of their number who was lying in the middle. An older man was bent over him, holding a curious instrument. Jess looked at Harrington.

"He's getting tattooed," he whispered. "It's a long and painful process. His friends watching here will probably be next."

Jess, taking shots of the solemn faces of the boys, was already forming captions in her mind. "An Iban boy on his way to manhood."

And so the afternoon went. By evening Jess was ready to put on her sarong and go to the river with the others. Fortunately, Thorpe was still busily engaged with the chief and she and Harrington spent a pleasant hour splashing about in the shallows.

She faced dinner with equanimity and the display of a

large row of human skulls with a placid smile. So these
men had once been headhunters, she told herself. In
actuality they were far less dangerous to her peace of
mind than the bronzed, rugged man who was her
employer.

After the meal and the display of skulls, they were
led into the cool inner room and shown to straw mats.
"Sleep well, Jess," said Thorpe as he settled on his mat.
"Tomorrow you'll get to see the real jungle. My friend
the chief is going to show us some pitcher plants."

"I'll be ready," replied Jess.

"Good." Thorpe turned his back to her and seemed
to relax instantly.

Jess, trying to get comfortable on the mat, found her
mind going again to her equipment. Everything had to
be right.

She feared that she would lie awake for long hours
again, but sleep overcame her quickly and the next
thing she knew someone was shaking her awake.

"Come on, Jess," siad Thorpe, his two-day growth of
beard giving his face a dark, piratical cast. "We're
going into the jungle."

"Yes, I'm coming." Jess, looking up into that dark
face, felt her heart pounding in her throat. How she
longed to reach up to him. For a long intimate moment
he stared into her eyes and then he turned away.

Jess fought to bring herself back to reality. This was
no time to be thinking of Thorpe's good looks or trying
to decipher the strange quality of his gaze. She must get
on her feet and moving.

Half an hour later Jess stood ready. Since their trip
would not be an overnight one, she had her case with
her equipment.

Thorpe gave her a curt nod and set off down the trail
behind the guide. With a wistful look at the women and

children playing in the river's shallows, she set out after him. The trail was narrow and so there was little chance for Harrington, directly behind her, to do much talking.

The trail began to get steeper but Jess managed to keep up the pace, and, when Thorpe turned to look at her, she returned his gaze evenly.

After about an hour's trek, Thorpe halted. The guide began to hack his way into the thick greenery. Thorpe followed and Jess was close behind, her hand already on the camera case.

Suddenly Thorpe halted again. He stepped to one side and pointed. Hanging from the trees were pitchers of various sizes and colors. They were similar enough to those Jess had seen in the Botanic Gardens to be recognized as pitchers, but she could tell they were not of the same variety.

The long, pod-like pitchers were topped by very tall scarlet collars.

"Nepenthes *veitchii*," said Thorpe. "They like to climb trees."

Some of the bigger pitchers were nearly a foot in length. Jess reached for her camera. "I want some close-ups, too," said Thorpe, "showing the insides."

Jess nodded absently, her mind on light meter readings and filters. She took shots from every conceivable angle, showing tiny pitchers with their mouths still sealed, slightly larger ones just open with a few insect victims, fully grown ones full of insect remains, and brittle ones, already deteriorating.

Projecting from the upper parts of the vine were delicate pea-size blooms arranged in spikelike racemes. They seemed to be of two distinct kinds. "What are these?" she asked.

"Those are really the flowers," explained Harrington. "Male and female flowers are quite different. The pitchers are actually modified leaves. That's why they change color as they do."

"Does anyone know *why* they trap insects?" asked Jess.

Harrington smiled. "It looks like it's caused by the lack of nitrogen in the soil. The years of heavy rains here have leeched away essential minerals. So the plants use the insects as a diet supplement. Much as we use vitamin pills."

He pointed. "The mouth of each pitcher produces insect-luring chemicals. When the unsuspecting insect comes along and tumbles in, it's lost. See these bristles? And the smooth waxy surface?"

Jess nodded.

"Claws, sticky pads, or hooks can't grip that surface. And if the victim were to make it up the slick sides, it would run into those bristles, an overhanging row of spikes, and be stopped dead."

Jess wrinkled her nose at the pun and turned to take shots of the contents of the well of one particularly large pitcher. Then she looked to Thorpe. "Are there any other shots you want?"

He shook his head. "No. Just get one of Harrington and me beside these. I've collected some seeds for the Botanic Gardens."

As Jess focused the camera on the two men who bent as though to examine the flower, her hand began to shake. She was not sure of the first shot and so she called, "Hold it. Just another for insurance." This time she managed to hold steady, though the effort of regarding Thorpe as just another subject for a photo was difficult.

"They used to call these 'monkey cups,'" said Thorpe pleasantly. "The natives claim that monkeys drink the fluid."

"And do they?" asked Jess.

"I once saw one doing so," said Thorpe. "Actually the liquid can be drunk by humans without causing them any trouble. Its taste resembles that of water from the great bamboos. Would you like to taste it?"

Jess was about to say no, but something about his look made her change her mind. "Yes," she said.

She really rather expected him to cut one of the bigger ones with its rather grisly remains of dead insects, but instead he cut a small one that had not yet opened its cap and so contained nothing but liquid.

She accepted it with a smile and drank it up. "It's not bad at all," she said. "Just a little warm."

Thorpe stowed the samples in his pack and turned to her. "We'd better head back. I want to return to Sibu tonight. Maybe we can find a hotel with a tub."

Jess flushed but smiled. "That's not necessary for me," she said. "I like the river."

It wasn't till after he gave her a rather curious look that she realized how her remark could be construed. If Thorpe was remembering the intimacy of that morning in the river, he might think she regretted Harrington's interruption. And she did not want him to think that—even though it was true.

But Thorpe said no more, just turned and followed the guide. The way back was easier since it was downhill. Soon they arrived at the longhouse.

"Get your gear," said Thorpe. "We'll eat some dried food in the speedboat on the way back to Sibu."

Jess nodded and went for her pack. Moments later she was passing the shallows where the same mothers and babies still splashed and played. A strange sort of longing crept over her as she paused a second to watch them. They were so obviously content, those women. Did they never have moments of regret, of yearning for something they didn't have?

Then she saw Thorpe and hurried toward the boat.

Soon the Iban longhouse was behind them. And as Jess munched on dried meat and fruit with the others, her mind moved ahead. Tomorrow they would go to Kota Belud and then to Mt. Kanabalu. It was that trip that she dreaded most—Kanabalu and its leeches. But she would handle it. She just would.

She dozed again as the speedboat raced down the river to Sibu. It was almost dark when they reached the city and Thorpe turned to her. "We can fly on to Tuaran tonight or we can stop here."

"We might as well go on," said Jess. "I'd like to spend a little while seeing the market at Kota Belud in the morning. That is, if we have time."

Thorpe nodded. "I'm to meet Anggau in late morning. So you should have some time."

"Good."

The lights of the city were going on around them as the car moved toward the airport. "Do you know anything about Sibu?" she asked Harrington.

He shook his head. "Afraid not. You've picked my mind clean of Sarawak facts."

"Sibu is Sarawak's number one trading city," said Thorpe. "It was originally a small Melanau village. Situated where the Rajang and Igan Rivers meet, it's a good spot for trade. A fort and a settlement were built here. Then seventy years ago the Foochow Chinese arrived. They took up trading, then planted rubber, got into growing pepper and the timber industry."

Jess nodded.

Then they had reached the airport and were busy getting aboard the Learjet. By the time they reached Tuaran and she tumbled into the car that was to take them to Kota Belud, she was moving in a kind of stupor. Somehow Thorpe managed to get in the middle, between her and Harrington. Deliberately she leaned her head against the window, but later, when she woke to find her head pillowed on Thorpe's shoulder, she was far too weary to protest and merely drifted back to sleep.

The morning sun coming through the hotel window roused her and Jess sat up startled. Her last real memory was of trying to keep awake. She must have fallen asleep and they had brought her to her room. She concentrated and finally retrieved a vague memory of being helped through the door, of Thorpe setting down her pack and saying, "There's a tub in the bathroom."

Yes, now she remembered. She had meant to take a bath, had even removed her clothes, but then the fatigue had been too much for her and she tumbled into the bed and was instantly asleep.

She glanced sharply at her watch; she didn't want to miss the *tamu* or market day. But it was still early. She could call Harrington. She reached for the phone.

Ten minutes later she emerged from the tub. It was nothing to compare to the one in Thorpe's house, but it did hold water. She dressed and hurried downstairs to meet Harrington for breakfast.

But the man waiting in the lobby was Thorpe. "Dick had some errands to run," he said. "I'll show you the market after breakfast."

Jess found herself nodding and wondering silently if Thorpe had invented Dick's errands. Certainly minutes ago Harrington had been free. Thorpe led the way to the dining area and they ordered breakfast.

"I brought my camera," she mumbled, patting the case. "I'd like to get some shots at the market."

Thorpe nodded. "There'll be a lot of local color there. Are you planning a photo story?"

Jess hesitated. "I really don't know. Sometimes I feel

like I've got the makings of one. And other times I just don't know. I'm used to working with wild animals and shooting a very specific sequence. These random shots are hard to coordinate."

Thorpe smiled. "I'm sure you'll come up with something eventually. Maybe when you have all the shots laid out I can see them."

"Maybe." This friendly attitude of his was a little disconcerting. Jess had no idea what she was eating. Thorpe's presence seemed to disrupt her senses. They ate their meal in silence, though occasionally Jess would glance up from her plate and find Thorpe gazing at her intently.

She was not in love with him, she told herself firmly. What she felt for Thorpe was physical attraction only. Lust, as they used to call it. Finally her plate was empty and they rose to go.

Under shady trees by the Tempasuk River the *tamu* was already under way. Women in colorful dress bore baskets of produce on their heads. An Indian medicine man charmed a cobra.

"After he finishes his act, he'll hawk his wares," Thorpe said. "Many people will think they are particularly good because of his control of the snake."

There were black caps on some male heads in the crowd. "Moslem Bajaus, once pirates," explained Thorpe. "They predominate on this part of the coast. Legend says they came originally from Malaya, descendents of sailors who were transporting a princess to her wedding with a Sulu sultan in the Philippines. When they lost the princess on the way, they decided it might be safer not to return home."

"They were rather wise men," Jess found herself saying and Thorpe nodded.

"Now they cultivate their padi fields, raise cattle, and

fish. They're very good at raising cattle and riding ponies, so good they're called the 'Cowboys of the East.'"

Jess, looking at the tough brown men, decided that they could probably handle anything American cowboys could.

"Kota Belud means Hill Fort," Thorpe went on. "It's really a cowboy town. This is the center of the pony and cattle raising industry. Look, there's a horseman in ceremonial attire."

Jess looked. The pony wore a harness strung with big bells around its neck. The horseman seemed to be wearing a long sarong of some purple material, a white shirt, and over this either one or two pieces of brightly patterned red material crisscrossed in the fashion of bandoliers.

But it was his headgear that most fascinated Jess. Another bright piece of patterned red material was wound around his head turban style. But this was unlike any turban Jess had ever seen. The folds stuck out stiffly and one shaded the wearer's face.

"A different kind of cowboy hat," cried Jess as she reached for her camera.

They continued to move along with the throng, Jess taking shots of whatever appealed to her. A dark-skinned girl, her jet black hair done up in a knot, sat on the bottom of a tall flaring basket that lay on its side.

"That's a *bongon*," said Thorpe. "A tree-bark basket. When she carried her produce to market in it, she wore it like a back pack."

Jess nodded. "A very useful piece of equipment."

They wandered up and down the aisles. Here were stacks of handwoven baskets that upside down looked almost like lampshades. Some were woven with flower designs, others with bright stripes of different colors.

"The women balance these on their heads," said Thorpe, "and carry produce in them."

The *tamu* seemed to have everything a person could want. Golden bunches of bananas, dried fish, fried cakes, mounds of green and yellow vegetables piled on fresh green leaves.

Jess drew in her breath as she spied a row of differend kinds of material.

"Handwoven," said Thorpe.

She turned questioning eyes to him. "It seems funny to see so many checks and plaids."

He smiled. "Perhaps that's a nice symmetrical pattern to follow."

Jess returned his smile. "Trust a man to take a practical point of view."

"Someone has to," he retorted with a wicked grin. "You women are such a romantic lot."

Jess did not answer this. Though she kept the grin on her face, she was conscious of a stab of pain. Was it her own streak of romanticism that made her long so for Thorpe? He was obviously a romantic figure. In her imagination she clothed him in tight-fitting breeches and an open vest that disclosed that hairy chest. With his growth of dark beard all he needed was a black patch over one eye. What a rakish pirate captain he would make! Feet planted firmly on the deck while he bellowed orders to his crew. And how he would have ravaged his female captives! Both physically and mentally, she thought with a grim smile.

"Jess, Jess," repeated Thorpe. "What diabolical thoughts are you brewing?"

She flushed and smiled. "I was just thinking. Nothing important."

He didn't look convinced.

"Does Sabah have any wild animals that Sarawak

doesn't?" she asked, hoping to distract him. The last thing she needed was to let him worm out of her something like that ridiculous fantasy. How he would laugh!

Thorpe frowned in concentration. "I believe there's a wild ox and a clouded leopard. Also on occasion we used to see the Sumatran rhinoceros. But that's extremely rare now, maybe even extinct."

They moved on again, Jess taking shots of the people offering their wares. Live chickens cackled loudly, birds sang in bamboo cages. Home-rolled cigarettes and jewelry were displayed on suitcase-top counters and more heaps of fruits and vegetables were spread out on the ground.

A young girl in a short black sarong moved gracefully past them. "A Kadazan girl," said Thorpe. "They live around Kinabalu. Those women over there with their heads draped in headcloths and chewing betel nuts are Bajau women."

Jess nodded. What would it be like to be such a woman, to squat all day in the sun or in the shade of an oiled-paper umbrella and offer the wares she had spent the week growing or making? She shook her head. It was impossible to imagine such a life. Without her camera— No, it wouldn't be life at all.

Thorpe paused before a heap of hollowed dried gourds. "See those?" he asked, pointing to a sheltered place where several tiny bamboo sticks lay. "They make little flutes out of them."

Jess paused a moment to marvel at the tiny things.

They had just about reached the end of the rows of displays when Thorpe consulted his watch. "I guess we'd better be getting back, Jess. But one more thing before we go. Look in that direction. Out over the city."

Jess looked. In the distance rose a great mountain, its granite peak towering up out of the tropical greenery.

"Aki Nabalu," said Thorpe. "The Kadazans named it long ago. 'Home of the spirits of the departed.'"

Jess gazed in awe for several minutes before she turned back. "Okay, I'm ready. Are we going to Kinabalu right away?"

He shook his head. "Not quite. I want to stop at the *kampong air* at Mengkabong on our way back to Tuaran."

"What is a *kampong air?*" asked Jess.

"A village built over water. Really rather pleasant to see. You can get some good pictures there."

As they moved back toward the hotel, Jess thought that it was fortunate that they had brought along the extra film. She would be sure to reimburse him for whatever she used personally, of course.

At the hotel Derek turned to her. "Be in the lobby in half an hour. Maybe I should have given you more time, but I figured you'd want to stay as long as possible at the *tamu.*"

"You were right," said Jess. "I'll be down on time. Thanks for the guided tour."

Thorpe smiled. "You're very welcome."

Thirty minutes was plenty of time for Jess to gather her things. She cast a wistful look at the tub before she left the room. It would have been nice to have one more leisurely soak. Well, she told herself, before too long they'd be through in the rain forest. Then she'd take a nice bath in that sunken tub back in Singapore before she left for the States. Suddenly Jess did not want to think about leaving Malaysia—or Derek Thorpe.

As she entered the lobby her first sight of the guide Anggau was not a particularly pleasant one. He was so heavily tattooed that it was difficult to see the man underneath. The expression on his face was one of hostility. Clad in a scanty scarlet loincloth, a feathered headdress, and fondling a huge ornamented *parang,* he looked the ultimate in savagery.

Jess smiled grimly to herself. Another headhunting wild man, no doubt. Would Thorpe never learn that she was not to be frightened by such juvenile tactics?

Still, when Thorpe arrived and said to the man, "Anggau, this is Miss Stanton. She takes pictures," Jess wanted to evade the gleaming black eyes that were turned on her.

"This one woman," said Anggau gruffly. "We go Kanabalu. Woman no go."

Not again, thought Jess with a sigh. The world seemed full of male chauvinists. But this time, surprisingly, Thorpe defended her. "This one goes. She takes good pictures."

Anggau shook his dark head, but he did not argue further. Thorpe was obviously the boss. Here as everywhere else.

Before long everything was loaded in the land rover. Jess, mopping her wet face with a handkerchief, thanked God for the waterproof tins that protected the precious film.

The drive to Mengkabong did not seem to take long. They passed through farm valleys, stands of rubber trees, wooded hills. And then they were there.

"This is a Bajau village," said Thorpe. "It's a perfect example of a *kampong air.* That's why I wanted you to see it."

Jess glanced at him. She couldn't help wondering at this new politeness, but he did not seem to notice as he continued to point out interesting things. "The houses are built on stilts high above the water, as you can see.

That makes them cool and free of mosquitoes. The dugout canoes are tied up under the houses at night. That metal-roofed building there is the mosque. It stands on an island in the center."

"Could we stop the car for a minute while I take a few pictures?" asked Jess.

"Of course," said Thorpe.

She almost glanced at him again, but he seemed entirely serious, no sarcasm evident in his voice. And then she was out of the car and lost in the scene before her.

The land sloped gently down to the lagoon where the stilted houses of thatch were scattered. She could almost hear the swish of the water against the pilings. How peaceful that would be at night. The wind whispered in the coconut palms above her head. And then down the dirt road came the sound of a mother crooning to her baby.

Jess stepped quickly back. This was what she needed to make her composition complete. A human figure.

She took several shots of the sarong-clad mother, the baby balanced on her hip, as she walked down the dirt road toward home.

Jess felt it was one of her best scenes and she was elated as she climbed back into the land rover. "Thank you," she told Thorpe. "This was great."

"I thought you'd like it," he said dryly. "Now we'll be getting on to Kanabalu. If we don't waste any time, we can set up our base camp before dark."

"That's fine with me," said Jess, determined to give him no room to accuse her of delaying anything.

In the hours that followed she had little time for concerted thinking. Every time she seemed close to a coherent plan for her photo story either Thorpe or Harrington interrupted her train of thought to point out something along the way. Finally she gave up. It would have to wait until she had the chance to think about it alone and unbothered.

"Of what tribe is Anggau?" she asked finally, aware that she must fill her mind with something in order to keep out visions of falling off a peak in Kanabalu or spoiling precious film.

"Anggau is a Murut, a man of the hills. His people are still animists—worshipping the spirits of the soil, the jungle, the river," said Thorpe from behind the wheel. "Too bad I haven't time to show you a village. Every one his its own *lansaran*, like a great trampoline. The Murut warriors, when filled with *tapia*, the local rice wine, spend their evenings singing, dancing, and leaping. Originally his people came from the hills. Traditionally they are great hunters and trappers. For a while disease took a terrible toll on them. But with government help—some land in the Keningau Valley—they made a comeback. They no longer get malaria. The valley was irrigated with government help and now they're holding their own."

He gave her a quick look. "They have a curious attitude toward death. Each corpse has his own little dwelling, equipped with implements, knives, a blowpipe. These are for use in the afterlife. And each little house is gay with bright colored flags.

"The Murut used to count their wealth in antique beads, old Chinese jars, and buffalo. A rather inconvenient medium of exchange, especially since the jars were big and difficult to lug about in the jungle and the buffalo live more than half wild."

"How would you like to go round up your money before you could go shopping?" asked Harrington.

Jess shook her head. "Not much. I'm beginning to appreciate more than one convenience of civilization."

Harrington rubbed his new beard. It was a warm golden brown. Jess wondered momentarily why a beard should make him look even more friendly while it made Thorpe look sinister and more mysteriously dangerous than ever.

She was letting her imagination run away with her, Jess thought grimly. Thorpe wasn't all that dangerous. And besides, he hadn't made any advances since that morning by the river.

It was late afternoon when they left the land rover and shouldered their packs and sleeping bags, and close to dusk when they finally stopped. Jess, who felt like she'd been following Thorpe for days instead of hours, slowly exhaled. So far she had made it. The sand flies were bad, biting stinging creatures with a grudge against mankind. Their bites were painful and annoying. But pain, thought Jess with a look at Thorpe, was relative after all. Far better to suffer a few insect bites than the agony of heart that loving Thorpe meant. Again she reminded herself that she did *not* love Thorpe. But the reminder did not work. And with a sigh she was forced to admit to herself that, call it what she would, Thorpe's attraction for her was stronger than ever.

The base camp was soon set up near the foot of the mountain. Jess marveled at the three-sided shelter of bark and grass put up by Anggau to keep off the rain. It did not keep off the sand flies, however, and Jess, feeling a mass of sweat and bites, longed for the comfort of a bug-free room.

But she rolled out her sleeping bag, and, after chewing some dried meat and fruit washed down by water from the little stream, stood surveying it. The bag would keep off the insects, but it was designed for far cooler climates and she would probably find it impossibly warm.

From beside her Thorpe spoke. "You'd be better to lie on top of the bag. The sand flies will soon be gone.

They don't fly at night. But the mosquitoes do. Did you bring a net?"

Numbly Jess shook her head. "No. You didn't mention—"

She thought sure he would take the occasion to give her a lecture on preparedness, but he simply smiled grimly. "You'll have to share mine."

Jess felt her heart rise in her throat. "I—I can't."

"You'll have to," he said firmly. "Mosquitoes carry malaria, among other things, and even though you've had your shots, you shouldn't be exposing yourself."

At her look of timidity he grinned, reminding her again of that image of him as a pirate captain. "I'm asking you to share my net, not my blanket. The net is transparent, you know."

Jess nodded and moved her sleeping bag so that it lay parallel to his. She left at least a foot of space between them, but Thorpe silently shoved them until they touched each other.

"My net is only so wide," he commented dryly. "It won't cover half the rain forest."

The shelter was very small, thought Jess. And surely with the others close Thorpe wouldn't try anything.

"In the morning before we go into the jungle, I'll get some Kadazans from a nearby village. They'll bring a couple of tents and some more supplies. They'll run the camp but they won't go any further up the mountain. It's still a sacred place to them." He looked at her. "Lie down. You need a good night's sleep."

Obediently Jess took her place on the sleeping bag and watched as Thorpe attached the net to a part of the shelter so that it fell over both bags. Then he carefully pulled it aside and crept in beside her.

Tired as she was Jess found it impossible to relax. He was too close and she was far too aware of it.

Finally he rolled over on his side and stared at her. In

the dim light of the moon she could see his eyes glittering. "Relax, Jess," he whispered. "This is not the place for it. I prefer to do my seductions with style."

She drew her breath in sharply, searching her mind for a caustic reply, but before she could find one, Harrington and Anggau entered the shelter.

Since Thorpe had put them in the middle of the shelter, the two latecomers had to move to either side. She heard the sound of Anggau grunting as he settled himself on the hard earth. No bag, no net, no nothing. This was Anggau's world and he was completely at home in it. He needed none of the trappings of civilization.

Harrington gave her a hurt look as he settled on her free side and she wondered what he was thinking. But he said nothing more than good night and that was all that she replied.

She lay in the darkness for a long time, trying to compose her thoughts so that she could sleep. She heard Harrington's breathing change as sleep overcame him. And then the rhythm of Thorpe's breathing changed too. Somehow, the knowledge that he was sleeping helped to relax her and finally she, too, fell asleep.

Some time in the night she wakened suddenly, startled by some sound in the jungle. For a long moment she lay trembling and, then, as memory of where she was returned, she felt the pressure of a hand on her hip. She was about to cry out when she realized that the hand was not moving. And Thorpe's breathing was still relaxed and regular. In his sleep he must have turned and now his hand rested on her.

A strange animal noise sounded in the jungle, but Jess was not frightened by it now. She felt somehow safe and protected. *I'm crazy,* she told herself. But nevertheless the feeling persisted. And with a sigh of contentment Jess shut her eyes again and slept, the last thing in her consciousness the pleasant awareness of Thorpe's protective closeness.

The harsh croaking call of a hornbill woke her and she saw that it was morning. Thorpe no longer lay beside her and she felt a curious sense of loss.

She felt somewhat rested, but the khaki clothes that she wore had been stained with sweat when she lay down in them. Now they were even worse.

From beside her Harrington spoke. "If you want to bathe in the stream, I won't peek."

Jess chuckled. "Thank you, Dick. You're a friend in need." She put aside the mosquito netting carefully and rose to her feet.

The place Thorpe had chosen was rather rocky, but Jess had no complaints about that. Insects didn't congregate on the rocks as they did in the damp forest.

A small stream trickled down by one side of the campsite, hardly large enough to sit in, yet the clear water could be scooped up.

Jess hurried out of her filthy clothes. The water felt delicious but she didn't linger with her washing. If Thorpe returned, he would not be so gentlemanly as Harrington. She was quite sure of that!

In a short time she was dressed in fresh clothes. She gathered up her dirty things and washed them in the stream.

When Thorpe and Anggau returned a short time later, followed by three husky Kadazans, she had rigged a rope line between two trees and her freshly washed clothes were drying. They would be wrinkled and stiff, but at least they would be clean.

Jess glanced nervously at Thorpe, but he said nothing about them, just immediately giving the natives their instructions and then turning to her to ask, "Are you ready?"

She nodded.

"Good. We'll leave now. Take some dried stuff along and we'll eat a regular dinner when we return at dusk. Agreed?"

"Agreed," echoed Jess and Harrington together. Who would dare not to agree, wondered Jess with a grim smile as she reached for her camera case?

And so the day began. She followed Thorpe and Harrington followed her and they set off up the mountain, munching the dried fruit Thorpe handed them.

At first Jess enjoyed the jungle around her, so green and lush. At the head of the line, wielding his *parang* with heavy grunts, strode the nearly naked Anggau. He seemed to be making a great deal of unnecessary noise. Jess was going to ask about it when the truth hit her. Anggau was deliberately warning any wild animals that might be lurking about that men were coming through. Jess smiled. The old Murut knew his way around the jungle, all right.

The rain forest grew denser and darker with each step. It was more like burrowing than climbing, thought Jess. When they had traveled some time, the only noise made by Anggau, they reached a stand of towering bamboo. The emerald green shoots, each four to six inches in diameter, grew in thick clusters. While Jess watched, Anggau whacked a shaft just above a joint and out poured a crystal-clear fluid.

The guide made a cut for each of them and Jess found the liquid cool and pleasant tasting. "It's quite germ-free," said Harrington as he finished. "The inside of a bamboo stalk is completely aseptic."

Then the bamboo slowly gave way to other vegetation. Under and around towering trees, lianas as thick as a man's leg writhed and twisted in their eternal search for sunlight. The dank vegetation seemed almost to be clutching at them like something out of a horror film.

And then the leeches arrived. From chinks in the humus or from under fallen leaves they came, hunching and lunging along like inchworms.

Jess barely stifled a scream as she noticed the first one on her boot and saw them moving on the ground all around her.

"Nobody knows for sure how they find us," explained Harrington. "Maybe the vibrations of our footsteps, our scent, our body heat, or maybe they can 'see' us. But they certainly are bloodthirsty little creatures."

Jess suppressed a shiver.

"Too bad you don't smoke," said Harrington. "A lighted cigarette touched to them makes the little devils loosen their hold. You mustn't try to pick them off, though. If you leave part of one in you, it's apt to get infected."

"The best thing," said Thorpe grimly as they moved along, "is to let the little devils gorge themselves. Then they'll fall off."

This time Jess did not succeed in suppressing her shiver of revulsion.

"Nobody ever died of leech bites," Thorpe continued. "And they get into you so smoothly you hardly feel it."

Jess wished she had brought a pair of gloves. But she had never gotten used to working in them. Even in the coldest of winters she had to strip off her gloves to take her shots.

She tried not to think about it, but it seemed that every inch of her body was exposed to these vile creatures and the thought made her almost ill.

Still she struggled along after Thorpe, determined not to give in to the queasiness in her stomach or the terrible pictures of blood-gorged leeches growing bigger and bigger that her mind insisted on flashing before her.

Suddenly Anggau stopped. Thorpe stepped aside. "Get some shots of these."

Jess looked at the series of knotty black-brown humps on the surface of a liana. They ranged in size from some as small as walnuts to others as large as cabbages.

"Young flowers," said Thorpe. "Not open yet."

He sliced into a large one with his bush knife.

Jess gasped at the exposed cross section of floral parts—all on a gigantic scale. A cluster of almost mature petals, speckled red and yellow, curled tightly around a lumpy yellow core.

"It was close to blooming," said Thorpe when Jess had finished shooting. "Anggau, find us a big one." Thorpe illustrated this request with a great circle of his arms.

The native nodded. "I find."

And so the trek began again. The jungle was steamy and Jess's khakis had been wet after the first half hour. But now it seemed to get worse. She wanted to gasp for breath and she was quite sure that there were leeches in her boots and trousers. She began to itch, too, but of course could do nothing about it.

Finally they stopped again. "I find," said Anggau proudly. "Big one."

Jess drew in her breath at the sight of it. On a mammoth vine grew a flower so large— "It really is as big as a washtub," she exclaimed.

Thorpe nodded. While Harrington gently raised two drooping petals on either side, Thorpe measured. "Twenty-nine inches," he said with a note of achievement in his voice. "That's the biggest we've found."

Jess stared at the gigantic flower. Its deep-set center

glowed yellow-orange, almost like the remembered coals of a banked fire in the ranch house in winter. The petals were leather-thick and several were already slightly beyond their peak, turning brown and flaccid.

The flower had no visible stem or leaves.

"Rafflesia is a parasite," explained Thorpe. "It has no leaves because it doesn't need them. It sucks its food through strands of tissue sunk deep into the host vine."

Jess took many shots, including one of Thorpe collecting the sticky seeds.

"No one knows exactly how the seeds get to new hosts," he continued. "Maybe they get caught in the fur of dining rodents and later fall off."

Jess took in this information silently. Certainly the flower was huge and interesting to see. But it was static; there was nothing intriguing about it like there was about the animals she loved or the people she had recently shot. The flower, she thought, had no personality. That was the crux of it.

Glancing at her watch, Jess saw that it was already well past noon. Thank God the way back to the camp was downhill. She was beginning to detect a weakness in her knees. And her stomach, which had not been treated well lately, was also complaining.

As they turned to go, she saw a leech on Thorpe's back and barely prevented herself from screaming. It seemed to grow visibly larger under her very eyes as it sucked his life's blood. She had to swallow twice before she could speak. "There's a leech on your back."

Thorpe shrugged. "He'll fall off when he's ready."

Jess gnawed her bottom lip to keep from crying out. She knew that she, too, had been bitten. Perhaps even now there were leeches on *her* back. It was only with the greatest effort that she could keep herself from retching.

On the way back to camp she tried to occupy herself

with thoughts of Montana, of sagebrush and buffalo grass, steers in the corral, the crisp cold of a winter morning, the deceptive smell of the chinook as its false spring warmth momentarily melted the frozen drifts.

And finally they reached the camp. The Kadazans had set up two small tents and the smell of something cooking came from the open fire. But by now Jess's stomach had ceased complaining. She only wished she could lie down somewhere and die. Every muscle and tendon in her body ached. Her khakis were wringing wet and even her hair, usually tight in its natural curls, hung lankly against her neck.

She went to a stream for a bucket of water and then asked Thorpe, "Which is my tent?"

"The one to the left. The natives have put your pack in it."

"Thank you."

Jess gathered her clean clothes from the line she had rigged and made her way into the tent, dropping the flap behind her.

No air would circulate with the flap down but at least she would have privacy. She had to get out of these filthy clothes and wash off the blood she was sure clung to her legs and ankles.

She stripped off her clothes and threw them into a pile. The leeches had worked their way between the laces of her boots, eaten their fill, and been squashed. She felt her stomach heaving but there was little in it to lose. At least there were no live leeches left, she thought wearily as she began to wash.

She finished washing and, wrapping herself in the sarong, lay down on her sleeping bag. It was beginning to get dark and the tent seemed cooler. She had no desire to eat, no desire to move. She was clean and bug-free and she wanted only to be left alone.

"Jess, I'm coming in." The interval between

Thorpe's announcement and his pulling aside the flap was so brief that she could only gasp a word of protest.

He held a lantern in one hand. It sent a strange glow over his bearded face and weird shadows on his sarong. "Well, Jess, on your feet. Time for inspection."

She struggled to her feet because she realized immediately how vulnerable her prone position left her. But she repeated, "Inspection?"

"Yes. I've brought the antiseptic for your bites."

Jess extended her hand. "I can put it on myself, thank you."

Thorpe shook his head. "No, you can't. There are places you can't see or reach."

Jess tried to summon some anger to fight him with but her fatigue was so great that she could scarcely stand.

"I'll start with your feet and legs," he said, setting the lantern on the floor.

The antiseptic stung, but after the initial discomfort, it seemed to relieve the itching. As Thorpe moved further up her legs, Jess grew more alarmed. What if—

But when he reached her knees, he stood up. "Take off your sarong," he said softly.

Jess's eyes widened. "No!" she whispered.

"You have bites on your arms. See? You probably have some on your back, too. Without the antiseptic they'll get infected."

"But—"

"Jess, I'm boss here. This is necessary. Besides," he said grimly. "There are four men out there and if you scream, Harrington, at least, will be here instantly."

Jess was silent. She couldn't do as he said and yet there was truth to his comment. She wouldn't be able to function properly if she got ill. And, said the little demon inside her, he had already seen her—the morning at the river.

Still she stood irresolute.

"Now, Jess." His eyes stared into hers and almost of their own volition her hands moved to the sarong and it fell to the ground.

"That's better," he said. "We don't want you to be infected."

And with a tenderness that she found quite surprising, he searched for and treated each bite.

Finally he set the antiseptic aside. "There, that should do it."

Jess knew she should reach for the sarong, but his eyes seemed to hold her. And then he took the one step that separated them and she was in his arms.

"N—" Her lips began to form the word, but he cut it off with his own, covering hers so skillfully that she could not have cried out. His hands on her back pulled her close against him, crushing her softness against his lean hardness.

She felt his chest hair against her naked breasts and a shiver went over her. His lips moved over hers, nibbling, teasing, setting her blood on fire. The pulse pounded in her throat as she opened her mouth to his, as his tongue gently mingled with hers. He set his teeth lightly in her bottom lip and the wild thing within her fluttered crazily.

She felt the strength leave her legs. This time there was not the slightest doubt in her mind. She could fight him no longer. Whatever he decided to do with her she was helpless before his power.

She clung to him, burying her hands in his curly hair, opening her body—and her soul—to his kisses. When he pushed her down on the sleeping bag and threw himself beside her, she had no thought of protest. She had no thought at all. Only feelings. Feelings that pulsed through her in a way she had never known.

And then suddenly he muttered a harsh curse and

stumbled to his feet. Without a word to her, he grabbed up the lantern and left.

As the tent fell into darkness Jess lay stunned. So much of her had been concentrated on her senses that for a moment she couldn't believe that he was gone. Then, finally, realization hit. He *was* gone and he was very angry.

She groped in the darkness for the sarong and used it for a cover. Why was he angry? she asked herself. He had wanted her, he had overpowered her with that fierce masculinity of his— And now he was angry. It didn't make any sense to her at all.

The tears rose then and she let them trickle unheeded down her cheeks. This assignment had been an awful mistake. She had been foolish to think that she could escape an expert like Thorpe. Even now her body remembered the touch of his hands.

With a sob she rolled over and buried her face. There was no use denying it any longer. She was in love with Thorpe. In love with a man who had an almost-certain fiancée and an absolutely-certain mistress. And, she told herself bitterly, I must be stark raving mad!

# Chapter 6

The next morning Jess took the trouble to eat a decent breakfast. She could not go trekking through the jungle all day on an empty stomach. Fortunately, the Kadazans had brought fresh supplies and one of the Kadazans proved to be a passable cook.

Jess ate slowly, giving her stomach a chance to work. She had avoided Thorpe's eyes when she left her tent that morning and he had not spoken to her. She had wakened once in the night to the feel of something against her cheek and realized that he had crept back in and put up his mosquito net. She recognized its distinctive texture. The tent was empty then, though, and she drifted back to sleep.

Now, sipping hot coffee, she pondered what to say to him. She wanted to thank him for the net, but she knew that if he looked at her, she would flush scarlet. And was he still angry with her?

The morning heat seemed particularly oppressive and Jess's khakis were already wet. Sometimes she wished she were a native. It would be so much simpler. But the thought of those leeches was always in her mind. And khakis, even if ineffectual, were better protection than a sarong.

"The going today will be rougher," said Thorpe, giving her a strange look. "We're going up near the summit. It's steep. Anggau will carry since we'll be out all night."

Jess nodded. She still did not trust herself to speak.

Soon they were on their way, but now the trail bent more steeply upward. Jess, thinking of the sharp outline of rock that she had seen before the clouds closed around the summit, shivered slightly. The peak was a long way up, over 9000 feet, and Thorpe had said the way was steep.

They hadn't been long on the trail when it began to rain, a cold drizzle that soaked to the skin and made sucking mud of the earth beneath their feet. Jess, shivering with the unexpected cold, was reminded of autumn rain in the States. But the cold seemed strange among the tropical greenness. All around were fascinating shrubs, vines, and mossy boughs, but Thorpe saw none of them. He moved stubbornly on.

The closer they got to the top, the slower Anggau moved. Jess welcomed the slower pace but she wondered at it. Finally Anggau stopped completely. "No go. Spirits angry. You have chickens? Eggs? We make sacrifice."

Thorpe shook his head. "I wasn't about to carry seven chickens and seven eggs all the way up here. Come on."

Anggau shook his head. "Woman bad. Make spirits angry. Make rain. Anggau no go."

Thorpe shook his head. "We need you. I told you we want to get to that rock before dark."

Anggau squatted defiantly, his pack sitting before him. "Anggau no go," he repeated firmly.

Thorpe gazed in exasperation at Harrington as though to say, "What next?"

Jess debated only for a moment. Then she moved

forward and swung Anggau's pack to her back. "Which way?" she asked Thorpe.

He gave her one surprised glance then led off up the trail, completely ignoring Anggau.

Some moments later Jess found the guide beside her. "Woman not better than Anggau," he said gruffly as he retrieved his pack.

The rain plastered their hair against their heads and dripped from their noses as they forced the jungle to let them through. The trail grew so steep it was like climbing a staircase.

It seemed to Jess that they had been climbing forever and that they would never stop. Her every thought was concentrated on putting one foot before the other, up and up, the mud pulling at her boots until she wanted just to lie down and give up.

But she didn't. She tried to beguile her mind with ideas for her photo story, with memories of the Montana hills, even with the recollection of being in Thorpe's arms. But even that did not work. Her abused and exhausted body kept clamoring for rest.

Finally, when she thought she couldn't take another step, Harrington spoke. "Time for a rest break, Derek. If you ever want to have me along again on one of these expeditions, it's *definitely* rest time."

Jess, casting him a grateful look, was surprised to see that Harrington looked exhausted, too. With his hair plastered wetly against his head, his shirt stuck to him, and rain dripping from his beard, he looked a sorry sight. Dear God, thought Jess, she must look horrible herself.

"Ten minutes," said Thorpe in a tone that brooked no interference.

Jess and Harrington sank down on adjoining rocks. "I'd lie down if it weren't for the mud," whispered Jess.

"And the leeches," replied Harrington softly.

Jess was momentarily startled. Her body had been in such agony that she had temporarily forgotten the little devils.

The ten minutes seemed like only ten seconds and then they were on their feet again, still moving ever upward.

It was late afternoon when they reached a large overhanging boulder that formed a kind of cave.

"Good," said Thorpe. "We made it."

Jess managed to keep going till she had laid out her bedroll and stowed her gear. Then she crumpled beside the fire. Thank God, she had not come on this expedition with new boots. Her feet were weary but they were not blistered.

Anggau paused to offer her a meal of tuna and canned peaches and she thought she saw a grudging respect in his eyes. She ate slowly, trying to put her mind on the food rather than on her weary body.

Thorpe remained silent during the brief meal and when it was finished they all turned to their sleeping bags. The great boulder that overhung the rock kept off the drizzle and Jess wished she had a nice dry suit of clothes to change into. But she didn't. Her body heat and the fire had partially dried them so she felt only damp as she crawled into her sleeping bag.

They had picked off all the leeches that were visible and the rain seemed to have discouraged many of them. Jess was actually too tired to care.

She was just falling off into exhaustion when a deep voice beside her said, "Sleep tight, Jess."

She did not open her eyes to see him, but she knew that Thorpe was spreading his bag beside her and she felt good about it. Then exhaustion overcame her and she slept soundly.

The sun had barely risen when Thorpe was rousing

them from their sleep. A hasty cup of coffee and a few dried figs and they were on the trail again.

The mountain was shrouded in mist, but at least the drizzle had stopped. Moss and air plants hung heavily from the gnarled, twisted branches of mountain oak and conifer. The ground was an almost knee-deep matting of soggy sphagnum, with here and there a lichened rock sticking out. There were banks of rhododendrons and other flowers that Jess didn't recognize, delicate beautiful flowers. Birds chirped somewhere in the jungle and from somewhere in the distance came the rumble of a waterfall.

Looking around her, Jess had to admit that the jungle was a beautiful place, lush and green. But from deep within her came a yearning for home, for the sight of brown sagebrush and buffalo grass, for the sound of chattering prairie dogs afternoon visiting outside their burrows. For something sane and sensible. For something *known*.

That was it, thought Jess. Montana could be every bit as dangerous as the rain forest. But the dangers at home were familiar ones. And there was no Derek Thorpe to complicate matters!

And then suddenly Anggau stopped, "Ah, good," he said.

The three of them crowded around to examine the pitcher plants. These were deep red-orange, their caps sometimes the same color, sometimes a pale green.

"These are Nepenthes *villosa*," said Thorpe. "Where is the new one?"

Anggau shrugged. "I see before. We find."

Jess, taking some quick shots before they moved on, noted how the rim of this species was deeply fluted, almost like corrugated cardboard. Something about them reminded her of pictures of the human heart that she had seen. The resemblance was probably caused by their shape, she thought, combined with their color and the peculiar fleshy-looking texture of this variety.

Then she was hurrying on after Thorpe and the others. Soon Anggau stopped again. This time some of the small pitchers were pale green. There was a short pause and Thorpe said curtly, "These are *gracilis*."

Jess, thankful that she was not the guide, followed as once more they moved on.

They trekked on for more than an hour before once again Anggau called a halt. This time the pitchers hung from a tree overhead. A very deep green, they lacked the barbed escape-proof rims of the others.

Thorpe shook his head. "These are *lowii*."

"Isn't it possible that we've discovered all the species there are?" asked Harrington reasonably.

"Anggau said he would show me a new species," said Thorpe stubbornly. "And I intend to see one. Today."

Jess, who had been rather sympathizing with Thorpe in his disappointment, now felt her feelings shift. It was stupid to go tramping about a rain forest all day, looking for a non-existent plant. She was getting tired of it.

But Anggau led off again and the rest followed. They had walked for some time again and Jess was beginning to feel very tired when she suddenly heard a shout from behind her.

Turning, she saw that Harrington had moved off into the jungle. "Derek," he called. "Look at this!"

Thorpe came pushing back past her so fast that he almost knocked her over. There was a startled exclamation from him and a garble of excited voices. By the time she got there the men were pounding each other on the back and shouting while Anggau stood looking on like an indulgent parent.

"What is the reason for all this rejoicing?" asked Jess dryly.

"Here." Thorpe pointed to a vine from which hung several pitchers of various sizes. They were different in coloring from the others and the pods were more elongated, but other than that they did not seem unusual.

Jess, taking shots from every angle, was vaguely aware of the discussion the men were having. But racemes and pistils were not familiar expressions to her. She finished the roll with a shot of the two, like conquering heroes holding aloft their prizes.

Finally they were on their way back down the trail. For some time Jess had been aware of a hazy sort of discomfort. She had attributed it to all the excitement and the exertion, but now the feeling grew.

They'd been walking for several more hours and Jess was to the point where every step was an effort of concentration. The jungle seemed to swim in a greenish haze, everything around her distorted and blurred. Resolutely she kept her eyes on the trail.

She was just tired, she told herself. But she would not say so. She would be all right when they got to the base camp. She would rest there.

And then suddenly, looming up from the forest beside her, shot a snake. She saw the cobra's inflated hood, the death's-head staring at her, and she screamed. She screamed again and again, until Thorpe slapped her sharply across the face. Then she fell fainting into his arms.

When she opened her eyes, he and Harrington were standing over her. "You're ill." Thorpe glared down at her. "Why didn't you tell me?"

Tears brimmed her eyes but she could not speak.

"You've picked up some kind of fever. Didn't you notice that you were sick?"

Jess shook her head. "I thought I was just—tired."

"Stupid," said Thorpe. "If you'd told me sooner, we might have stopped it. Well," he shrugged. "We have to get back to camp."

The two of them helped her to her feet and immediately the world began to revolve. "I—" she began and passed out once more.

When Jess regained consciousness again, she realized that she was being carried. Thorpe was carrying her along the trail they had cut.

She began to protest and was quickly silenced. "You've made enough trouble," he said curtly. "Besides, a kitten like you doesn't weigh much."

"My camera?"

"Anggau has it. Relax."

There seemed nothing else to do and Jess slipped into a half-doze. From time to time she realized that she was being shifted from one man to another, but increasingly she seemed to be floating in a strange greenish haze.

She woke when they laid her in the tent and Thorpe brought cool water from the stream to bathe her.

"So hot," she mumbled through dry swollen lips.

"Easy, kitten, easy." His voice was so gentle that even in her half-conscious state she noted it. He bathed her fevered body and spoke to her softly. "Easy, Jess, easy. I'm here. Nothing can hurt you now." Soon Jess floated back into that hazy green oblivion.

This time it was frightening. Lianas hanging from mist-shrouded trees were suddenly transformed into great cobras with black eyes that gleamed at her evilly. And dropping from the trees by the hundreds and thousands came bloodthirsty leeches until they covered her whole quivering body.

Jess's screams rent the night air. Thorpe was there instantly, trying to calm her.

"Leeches, leeches," she sobbed. "Can't stop them."

"Jess, Jess." His voice came to her as from a great distance. "There are no leeches. It's the fever. You're delirious."

She twisted her head from side to side. "No! Leeches, leeches everywhere."

"I'm taking them off, Jess," he said softly. "I'll get them. Every one. Don't worry. I'll keep them off. You just rest. Do you hear me?"

"Yes." The word was a long drawn-out sigh of relief. If Derek said he would get rid of them, then he would. Derek could do anything.

When Jess opened her eyes again, she saw the peach-colored walls of her bedroom in Thorpe's Singapore house. She felt curiously weak and for a moment she thought she was dreaming. Then she attempted to move her head and was startled to find how weak she really was.

From across the room Thorpe came striding. He still wore his growth of jungle beard, but she knew that this was no dream. "What happened?"

"You had a jungle fever. It was pretty bad there for a while."

"But how did I get here?"

"We carried you out. You're a lightweight anyhow."

"My camera! The film!"

Thorpe scowled. "They're perfectly safe. You might give some consideration to the fact that you've just come out of a dangerous jungle fever. You can think about the film later."

"I'm sorry to have been such a burden to you," Jess said. "I didn't know it was a fever."

Thorpe shrugged. "You did your job. And you were certainly easier to carry out than a big hulk like Harrington. Now sleep. You need the rest."

Jess nodded. "I will. And thank you for taking care of me."

Thorpe shrugged again. "I told you before. I always take care of my people."

And then he was gone, striding from the room so quickly that even if she had had the strength to throw her pillow as she felt like doing, it would have been too late.

For a few moments there she had hoped that his actions meant something special. But she was just another one of his 'people,' someone the great patriarch felt responsible for.

The tears brimmed over from her eyes and rolled down her cheeks. It was thus that Ah Cheng found her minutes later. "Miss no cry," she said cheerfully. "Be better soon. Tomorrow I cook American breakfast. You eat, yes?"

Jess nodded. "Yes, thank you. I—I'm sorry to have caused you so much trouble."

"What trouble?" asked Ah Cheng. "Master Derek, he take care you. No let Ah Cheng do anything." A strange look crossed her face. "You need husband. I look for go-between."

"No. Ah Cheng, I can't. I can't just marry anyone."

"Find good man. Have money. You be better."

"No, Ah Cheng." Jess struggled to sit up. "Money has nothing to do with it. It's—" Her voice broke. "It's love that's important. Only love."

"Marry first, love after," said Ah Cheng soberly.

Jess shook her head. "It's too late for that, Ah Cheng. Too late."

The Chinese woman said no more, simply fluffed up Jess's pillows. "You rest now."

"Yes." Jess fell back among the pillows. She was really exhausted and soon sleep overcame her again.

When she woke the next time, she felt somewhat stronger. And lying there in that half-doze between sleep and waking, she searched her memory. There was the vivid picture of the cobra hissing at her and then vague bits and pieces, memories of being carried by Thorpe, by Harrington. Memories of Thorpe bathing her feverish body.

She shivered as she recalled the delirious dreams of leeches that had terrified her and resounding through her memory came the echo of Thorpe's deep voice. "I'll keep them off you, Jess. Relax." And even in her delirium she had trusted and believed in him.

She smiled grimly. The fantasy of a lovesick woman. That's what it had been.

And yet she had to admit that Thorpe *had* taken care of her. For whatever his reasons.

She moved restlessly on the silken sheets, thinking of the film in the waterproof cases. She must hurry and get well. Then she could develop the prints for Thorpe and get out of Singapore. It was stupid to hang around and be continually hurt. And there would be no more fooling herself that she could withstand Thorpe. That was just courting disaster. The sooner she left Singapore—and Thorpe—behind, the better.

The tears were about to overflow again when Ah Cheng pushed open the door. "You see visitor?" she asked. "Miss Haviland stop. See how you are."

Jess toyed with the idea of saying that she was too tired. The last person in the world that she wanted to see was Haviland Phillips. But if Miss Phillips wanted to make a duty call, then she might as well get it over with. "Send her in," Jess told Ah Cheng, hoping that she kept the resignation out of her voice.

Ah Cheng nodded.

Moments later Haviland Phillips entered. In her yellow linen dress she looked as cool and chic as ever as she pulled up a chair. "I'm glad to see that you're better," she said.

"Thank you," replied Jess, wondering why Haviland Phillips should feel any concern for her welfare. The answer was soon forthcoming.

"Dear Derek has been so upset. Those pictures mean a lot to him."

"I'm sure they do," said Jess stiffly. "But they are quite safe."

Haviland Phillip's perfectly painted mouth pouted. "We won't know that till we see the prints, now will we?" She shook her well-coifed head. "Poor Derek is a nervous wreck with this waiting. Thank goodness, when we're married this sort of thing will end. I can't imagine why anyone should want to go marching about in that horrid old jungle."

Jess, who had been waiting patiently for the visit to end, felt her heart rise up in her throat. "When Derek and I are married," Haviland had said. Grimly Jess interrupted Haviland's tirade against the wicked old jungle. "I'm terribly afraid I'm going to be sick," she said. "If you'd just get Ah Cheng."

Haviland Phillips paled and jumped to her feet. "Of course, of course," she cried as she hurried out the door.

Jess dissolved into half-hysterical laughter that turned into bitter tears. Well, now she knew how to get rid of dear Miss Phillips.

By the time Ah Cheng appeared she was wiping her eyes. Tears were of no use in this case.

"You sick?" inquired the old woman.

Jess smiled. "Miss Haviland's visit was tiring me and so I told her I felt ill."

Ah Cheng's wrinkled face creased in an appreciative smile. "I never see Miss Haviland move so fast."

Jess nodded. "I think I'll rest some more." She felt suddenly exhausted. So Derek Thorpe was going to marry Haviland Phillips. So what else was new? She had known that all along.

She slid down the pillows and tried to relax, but it seemed impossible. She tried to focus on her photo story, but nothing seemed to work. The image of Derek Thorpe, bearded and dark, kept intruding into her consciousness. He smiled at her, that grave mysterious smile that did such strange things to her.

And then the misery she had been holding down surfaced. How could Derek marry Haviland? How could he marry *anyone*? Surely she had meant *something* to him. Why had he taken care of her like that? Of course, he had desired her. That was clear enough from the first. He often desired women—and went after them. He had intended to use her, she thought bitterly. As he had undoubtedly used many other women. But that didn't explain his tenderness when she had been so ill. The whole thing was very confusing. She was just too tired to think about it anymore.

She had finally slipped into a fitful kind of sleep when the slight sound of the door opening wakened her. "You sleep?" asked Ah Cheng softly.

"No. What is it?"

Ah Cheng's face reflected her disapproval. "Helen Cheong here. Maybe you no see her."

Jess shook her head. "No, Ah Cheng, I'll see her. I might as well get it over with."

Once more Jess pulled herself erect in the bed. She hoped no more of Thorpe's women would stop by to establish their positions.

Helen Cheong was as lovely as ever, her shining black hair coiled against her smooth tan neck, her voluptuous body sheathed in a cheongsam that fit like a second skin. She barely smiled as she settled into the same chair that had held Haviland Phillips. "I've come to talk to you," she said briskly.

Jess contented herself with a quiet, "Oh?"

"I hope you don't think that you mean anything to Derek," she began.

"Of course not," returned Jess icily.

"Good. Because you don't." Helen said this calmly and coldly.

"I am quite aware of that," replied Jess, holding on to the anger that kept her desolation at bay. "But what about Haviland Phillips? She and Mr. Thorpe plan to marry."

Helen shrugged. "That one is a painted doll." She glanced at the nightstand where Jess's ivory lady stood. "She has no more feelings, no more warmth, than that statue. Me. I am what Derek wants. I am all woman." The Eurasian girl's dark eyes gleamed.

"So you don't mind if he takes a wife. What about other women?"

Helen's face flushed. "There will be no others," she said darkly. "I'll see to that."

Jess shook her head. "I think you're wrong, Miss Cheong. Very wrong. With Derek Thorpe there will always be others."

Helen Cheong's beautiful dark lips tightened into a thin line.

"And now," said Jess evenly, "since you have spoken your piece, kindly take your leave. If you love Derek Thorpe, you have my sympathy."

Helen Cheong laughed as she got to her feet. "Love?" she said harshly. "Who said anything about love?"

And then she was gone, leaving behind the lingering scent of her heavy perfume and a sour taste in Jess's mouth. Well, it was poetic justice, she supposed, that neither Haviland Phillips nor Helen Cheong loved Thorpe. Especially since he too knew nothing of the meaning of the word.

She was wondering whether her legs would hold her if she ventured out of bed when Ah Cheng came back, her eyes sparkling. "Helen Cheong very angry," she announced. "What you say her?"

Jess smiled. "I just gave her some advice."

"She no like," said Ah Cheng with what almost sounded like pleasure. "That one self-combed. No good for Master Derek."

Jess decided that it was wiser just to remain quiet.

Ah Cheng bustled about, plumping up her pillows and adjusting curtains. "You have another visitor," she said finally.

Jess sighed, her mind suddenly presenting her with a line of women that stretched into infinity. "Who is it this time?" she asked wearily.

"Mr. Harrington."

"Oh!" Jess brightened immediately. "Where is he?"

Ah Cheng regarded her closely. "He wait till I call. You want comb hair, wash face?"

Jess shook her head. "Of course not. I'm quite presentable."

Ah Cheng nodded and went out. Moments later Dick Harrington stood beside her bed. He had shaved off his growth of jungle beard and his eyes held deep concern as he gazed down into hers. "Jess, you gave us quite a turn."

"I assure you I didn't do it on purpose," she said brightly.

He took her hand between both of his. Jess felt a sudden pang of embarrassment and quickly withdrew it. "Sit down, Dick. Be comfortable."

He nodded and took the chair beside her bed. "I'm glad to see that you're feeling better. We were really worried about you."

"It was just a fever," said Jess.

Harrington gave her a grave look. "In the jungle there is no such thing as 'just a fever,'" he said grimly. "You really should have mentioned it as soon as you felt it."

She shook her head. "I know. But I didn't realize I *was* ill. Derek was driving us so hard. I thought it was just exhaustion."

Harrington frowned. "I've never seen him drive that hard. He almost did me in."

Jess nodded. "I've done a lot of wilderness hiking. Really I have. But that jungle—" She winced. "Sorry I did all that screaming about the snake."

"You were already half-delirious," he said smoothly. "You weren't responsible. The whole thing was Derek's fault." His voice rose. "He had no business being so tough on you."

To her surprise Jess found herself defending Thorpe. "He just wanted to prove his point. And I did goad him. I kept claiming I could do anything a man could."

"And you did," said Harrington.

"Until I got sick." Jess smiled but Harrington did not smile in return. His frown deepened.

"A man might have gotten sick, too. You needn't make excuses for him. Derek behaved very badly. He set out to make the whole trip as difficult as possible for you."

Jess shook her head. "I don't think he meant to be deliberately cruel."

"Well, he was!" Harrington seemed to be getting angrier. "Look at that business about the monkey meat."

Jess frowned. "I behaved like a baby. I shouldn't have let him get to me like that."

Harrington scowled. "You should be angry with him, Jess."

She shook her head. "But I'm not."

"I know—" Dick began and just then the door opened to admit Thorpe.

Jess colored as though they had been caught outright talking about him. He had shaved off his dark beard and changed his clothes. His shirt was of a particularly lovely shade of dark red. Perhaps it was the reflection from it that seemed to give added warmth to his eyes as he looked at her. "I hear you've been having visitors."

"Yes." Jess, seeing his eyes on the front of her gown, a gown which was quite high cut and opaque enough to satisfy a grandmother, fought a wild urge to clutch the sheet and pull it up over her.

"I hope they haven't tired you," he said curtly, with a purposeful look at Harrington.

Jess sprang to his defense. "Of course not. Anyway, Dick just got here."

The two men exchanged glances and Jess shivered. There was something hanging in the air between them, some terrible tension that she could not define.

Harrington reached for her hand and pressed it. "I'll stop in later. See how you are."

"That'll be nice, Dick. Take care."

She did not want to see him go. There was something about the set of Thorpe's mouth that warned her of a coming storm.

Harrington turned again at the door and smiled. Then he was gone.

Regretfully Jess looked back to Thorpe. He was regarding her critically.

She felt like squirming under his cold gaze. Finally she could stand it no longer. "Why do you stare at me like that?" she cried.

He smiled grimly. "I'm trying to understand you."

"That's hardly necessary. I'll be leaving soon. Anyway, I'm the one who's bewildered."

"Oh?" He raised a dark eyebrow. "What about?"

"What has happened between you and Dick?" she asked. "There's something wrong between you."

"Nonsense." Thorpe glared at her. "What did Harrington tell you?"

"He didn't tell me anything," said Jess, deciding quickly that he needn't know about Dick's accusations against him. "But you could cut the air in here with a knife."

"As close as you are to Harrington," said Thorpe sarcastically, "I suggest you ask him."

Jess felt her temper rising. "I don't see that it's any business of yours how 'close' I am to anyone!" she flared, the memory of the women's visits lashing her temper higher. "The fact that you employed me to shoot some photos doesn't give you the right to pry into my affairs. Affairs of the heart are not your business."

He continued to glare down at her.

"And you needn't play the Great White Father with me either," she cried, returning the glare.

Surprisingly he did not shout back. "I was only trying to help. Harrington is not the man for you."

This angered Jess even further. "What do you know about it anyway?" she demanded hotly.

For a long moment he stared at her and then he sat down on the bed abruptly and pulled her into his arms. It was done so swiftly that she had no chance to complain. She was crushed against his powerful chest, crushed and kissed so thoroughly, so completely, that for long moments all thought was suspended.

When he released her, she fell back, shaken, among the pillows.

"There," he said triumphantly. "You need a man

who can kiss you like that. Someone who will waken the woman in you."

In the silence Jess could hear herself fighting for breath. Without thinking, she drew back her hand and connected with his cheek. She was still weak but her anger had given her strength and the marks of her fingers stood out on his cheek. For a moment she thought he would grab her and shake her and her heart thudded in her throat. Then from somewhere she gathered the strength to reply. "I'm sorry to undermine your confidence in yourself," she said with all the ice she could put in her voice. "But you are quite mistaken. I do not need an arrogant, overbearing tyrant who thinks he can *force* a woman to love him—a conceited braggart who has women running after him because of his wealth and power."

He stood then and she saw his hands clench into hard fists and his face grow startlingly white as a telltale muscle in his jaw twitched. He stood glaring down at her and the tears rose to her eyes as she was torn again by her longing for him. Helplessly she watched as he stalked out. Dear God, she thought, how was she ever to get over loving him?

There was no answer to that—neither that day nor in the days to follow as Jess grew gradually stronger.

Punctually every day Thorpe arrived, inquired politely after her health, and departed. There was nothing *wrong* with the way he treated her. Certainly it was good to be treated with respect. And yet, he seemed very far away—a distant stranger whose eyes never seemed to really see her.

Harrington came, too, of course, and he and Ah Cheng spent long hours talking with her.

But one day before she had fully recovered, Harrington did not come and Ah Cheng had to make a trip to town for groceries. So Jess was left to her own devices. The novel she was reading seemed shallow and flat. She moved restlessly on the bed, reached for her clipboard and pad and began to scribble captions for her photo story.

But nothing seemed to come right. Her memories of the shots she had taken were growing vaguer and vaguer. If only, she thought angrily, looking toward the closet where the film and equipment had been stored, she could *see* the prints.

She was better; her strength had returned. She was using the tub by herself. There was absolutely no reason why she couldn't get up and start putting together her darkroom.

Feeling like a guilty child, she crept from the bed. She decided against dressing since she didn't intend to leave the room. The walls tilted a little as she first moved but actually she felt better to be up and about. She'd been too long in bed.

Soon she was happily engaged in clearing a space in the roomy closet. Fortunately, everything had been brought to her room on their return. She was so happily engaged that she didn't hear the door open softly, as it might if someone thought she were sleeping. And then a deep voice boomed out. "Just what do you think you're doing?"

For a moment Jess was paralyzed, standing there in her gown like a little girl caught with her hand in the cookie jar. Then she forced herself to straighten and face Thorpe. "I'm setting up my darkroom," she said, trying to keep the defiance out of her voice. There was no point in angering him any further.

"I see." His voice was deadly cold. "Didn't I tell you to stay in bed?"

"Yes, but—" For some reason the words deserted her. And in spite of her protests, she *felt* guilty.

"Back in bed," ordered Thorpe.

"I'm not a child," she cried angrily. "I'm perfectly capable of taking care of myself."

"I think not," he said flatly. And then, before she realized what he was doing, he crossed the room and scooped her up in his arms.

"Derek, put me down!"

He ignored her flailing arms and legs and carried her to the bed where he dumped her unceremoniously. "You will stay in bed until you're entirely recovered."

She struggled to a sitting position. "I want to get my pictures developed. And I'm perfectly all right now."

Grimly Thorpe crossed the room and gathered the cans of film. "You'll get these back when *I* say so," he declared curtly. "And not before."

This time Jess almost threw the pillow. If he hadn't been carrying the precious film— And then as the door closed behind him, she sagged back against the pillows. Angry as she was, she felt a curious lilt of relief. This was the old Derek. She knew how to deal with him, how to exchange angry words.

But the new one, the soft-spoken, incessantly polite man who inquired so solicitously about her health—this Derek Thorpe she did not know how to cope with at all.

Every comment she made during his brief daily visits was acquiesced to. Inevitably—and irrationally—she was treated with that distant politeness. It was enough to make her scream.

In the days that followed, however, Jess did not scream. Eventually Thorpe let her out of bed. Then he let her set up the darkroom. And finally came the afternoon when she could see the finished prints. She could see quite clearly how her photo story would come out and she was planning to send out a query as soon as she returned to the States.

The pictures were remarkably good, all of them, and

Jess felt a justifiable pride. But that pride was tinged with sadness. For a finished assignment meant leaving Singapore—and Derek Thorpe.

She was considering this when Harrington arrived. His response to the photos was enthusiastic, to say the least. "These are really great, Jess. The best we've ever had." He beamed at her.

Jess smiled in return. "I'm glad. Now Derek ought to be satisfied. I did my job and I did it well."

A shadow crossed Harrington's face and was quickly gone. "Want to take a walk in the garden?" he asked. "It's cooling down."

"Sure."

They stepped out through the French doors, shutting them carefully.

There was silence between them for some moments as Harrington led her deeper into the garden. Then suddenly under the shade of a flowering tree he turned and took her in his arms.

His kiss was gentle and tender, and somehow filled with longing. Tears rose to her eyes as he released her. "I love you, Jess," he said softly. "I want to marry you."

Jess swallowed over the lump in her throat. "I care about you a great deal, Dick," she said. "But I can't marry you. I don't love you—in that way."

"But you like me," he said. "You could learn to love me."

Jess, thinking of Ah Cheng, smiled. "I'm sorry, Dick, but my career—"

"You could go anywhere you want. I'd go with you." His eyes met hers. "You've never asked so I don't know if you're aware, but I can give you anything you want. I have the money."

A sob caught in her throat. "Oh Dick, I can't. I just can't."

He bowed his head. "I know. It's Derek. You're in love with Derek."

When she didn't answer, he went on. "I knew it. But I had to try. I've never met a woman like you."

Jess reached out to pat his hand. "I'm not all that unusual, Dick." The image of Haviland Phillips crossed her mind. "Perhaps you've just been meeting the wrong kind of woman."

He frowned. "I think not. I think you've fallen for Derek's well-known charm, that's all. Well, I hope you enjoy being part of the gang." And before she could reply he was gone.

She made her way slowly back to the room. There was no hope for her with Thorpe; she knew that. She could never shine in society like Haviland Phillips. And she hadn't the necessary skills to replace Helen Cheong.

And so, by dinner time, as she waited for him in the foyer, she had herself as composed as possible. She would give him her prints, get her check, and go home. She felt a sudden longing for Montana.

The door opened and Thorpe entered. "Good evening, Jess," he said with that studied politeness that seemed so unreal.

"Good evening. Look, the pictures are all done."

"Bring them to the office, please," he said. And Jess followed, her enthusiasm further dampened.

He spread them out on a long table and spent a good deal of time studying them. She watched his face, but, dark and impassive, it told her nothing.

Finally, when she thought she could stand the suspense no longer, he spoke. "They're very good, Jess. Thank you."

And that was all he said. Jess did not know exactly what she had expected, but it had been more than that.

"Thank you," she said dully. "If you'll just give me

my check, I'll head back to the States, get out of your way."

For a moment he stood silent, then he turned to face her. "I'm afraid I have another favor to ask of you."

"What is it?" asked Jess, trying to match his polite tone and failing.

"I'm giving a party to celebrate the new pitcher plant find. My friends would like to meet the photographer and of course Dick will be here." He watched her closely.

Jess hesitated. She knew it was dangerous to stay around Thorpe. Although he no longer seemed to be interested in her as a woman, in certain ways that made her pain even more unbearable. But it would look strange, especially after her illness, if his photographer departed so soon. "When will it be?" she asked.

"This coming Friday," he replied. "I've invited the Director of the Botanic Gardens. He'll announce the name of the new plant. Some other plant people are coming. Some of my friends. It means a lot to me to have you there." He refused to meet her eyes as he said this, but she realized quickly that he would lose face if she left before the party.

"All right," she said slowly. "I'll stay. But I want my check the next morning. I'll book my flight back home."

"I'll give you your check now," said Thorpe, moving toward the desk. "I trust you not to run out on me."

"Thank you." There was no sarcasm in his voice and none in her reply.

As he took out his checkbook and began writing, Jess looked around the room. So much had happened in the few weeks since they had first met in this room. So very much.

He rose and brought the check to her. "Thank you, Jess. You did a good job."

This was the time to say, "As good as any man," and she said it.

But instead of laughing or even glaring at her, he simply nodded gravely. "As good as any man."

And Jess had no reply. This was not the Thorpe she knew. It was like some vital part of him was missing.

It was like that during the days that followed. Thorpe was inevitably polite and gentle. He asked after her health and made general conversation, but it was as though he were a copy, a not-quite-complete-copy, of the real Derek Thorpe. Jess, nursing a breaking heart, tried to act nonchalant and felt she was failing.

And then Friday night arrived. Rummaging in her closet, Jess pulled out the cream-colored dress. Its scooped neckline and wide full sleeves were still not her style, but she was swept by a sudden urge to look very feminine. Once, at least, let him see her looking good.

When she stood before the mirror, she felt rather daring, but later standing in the huge living room, she felt more like a small child pretending to be grown up. Haviland Phillips, her golden beauty burnished to a high gloss by the ministrations of some salon, arrived in a dress of deep blue silk that could only be an original and wearing diamonds that must be worth thousands.

Jess had barely recovered from the sight of her and the sickening way she clung to Thorpe, when the door opened to admit Helen Cheong. Her tight-fitting cheongsam of burnt-orange was just the right color to set off her golden skin. As she moved gracefully across the room, Jess noted that even in walking Helen seemed to give off vibrations. Men turned to stare after her—as Jess was quite sure the woman expected.

She watched as Helen, ignoring Haviland Phillips, reached up to kiss Thorpe. The two women glanced briefly at each other, but neither seemed particularly distressed. As Thorpe led the two toward his library,

Jess could only turn away. There he was—Derek Thorpe—with his mistress on one arm and his future wife on the other. And they gave every sign of being a happy threesome!

Jess shivered. The thought of marriage without love had always been anathema to her. But both Haviland and Helen seemed quite capable of it. Though Haviland's liaison with Thorpe would have the blessings of society, it would be every bit as mercenary as Helen Cheong's. Both women wanted the things Thorpe could give them. They had no inkling of love.

Jess wandered around the room, stopping to talk to Harrington, whose eyes held hurt but whose voice was friendly, accepting the compliments of those who admired the photo display, trying to look happy while her heart was slowly breaking.

Finally she could stand it no longer and she slipped out and made her way toward the kitchen. Since her flight left early in the morning, she would just use this time to tell Ah Cheng goodbye. A lump rose in her throat at the thought that tomorrow night she would no longer be in Singapore.

She stopped at the kitchen door to wipe aside the tears that had sprung to her eyes. And then she heard Ah Cheng's voice. "We need many cakes, much, much food."

They were planning some kind of party. "Biggest feast ever," said Giok Leng. "Singapore never see like. Too bad no red sedan chair. I like."

Ah Cheng snorted. "Maybe no sedan chair. But biggest wedding we ever see."

Jess turned away from the door with a stifled gasp. They were planning a wedding! A big wedding!

She sobbed as she groped her way to the veranda and out into the night. Ah Cheng and her husband were discussing the wedding of Derek Thorpe and Haviland Phillips! They had to be.

The garden seemed very quiet and Jess stumbled toward its center. She had to find a place to hide, a place where Thorpe couldn't find her. She had known this was coming sometime, even sometime soon. But she had thought that by then she would be far away, busily wiping all memories of Derek Thorpe from her consciousness.

She found the stone bench and sank down on it. Surely he would not be announcing his engagement tonight. Not without warning.

And yet— What did he know of her true feelings for him? She had succumbed to his kisses and physically he must have felt her near-surrender. But verbally she had refused to acknowledge his pull on her. And, after all, her response to him had been that of any normal woman. As far as he could know she had enjoyed his kisses and that was it.

Suddenly she could sit still no longer. She must move around; she'd always been able to think better on her feet. She had to get away without Thorpe suspecting the true extent of her feelings. How amused he would be to discover that he had made such an unlikely conquest!

She got to her feet and began to pace back and forth. Obviously she could not hide out here forever. If Thorpe intended to make an announcement, then she must be there, ready to give her congratulations. Otherwise it would look strange, not only to Thorpe, but to his friends.

She wiped at her cheeks. She would go back to her room—she could get in from the veranda—and wash up. Then she would go back to the party and be cheerful. She would endure what she must. At least she still had her pride.

Hoping no one had noticed her absence, she increased her pace to almost a run. Now it became imperative to get back there before he made the announcement.

She rounded a bend in the dark and ran heavily into a male chest. The moment his arms went around her, she knew who it was and she struggled to release herself. But Thorpe simply held her.

"You shouldn't have left the party," he said softly. "After all, it's your party too."

Jess was near hysteria now. It was more than she could bear to be so close to him, to want to cling to him, and to know that it was useless. In her agony she struck out wildly, beating against his chest with her fists.

"Jess! Jess! Stop it." He shook her.

"I want to go home," she cried, the tears streaming down her face. "Let me go."

He pulled her then, in spite of her resistance, into his arms and kissed her long and soundly. Her mind told her to resist, but her body was powerless against him.

When he released her mouth, she was clinging to him weakly. "Now," he said. "Do you still want to go home?"

What gall the man had, thought Jess, summoning her strength. What colossal gall! "I don't play around with engaged men," she said stiffly.

He smiled, one finger tracing the outline of her stubborn chin. "I'm not engaged."

How *could* he be so perfidious? she asked herself. "You soon will be."

He stared at her for so long that she began to struggle again. But then he clasped her close. "Don't you know by now, kitten," he said against her hair, "that if *you* won't have me, I'll never be engaged?"

The air left her lungs suddenly and the world tilted

dangerously. Was it possible that the fever had re-curred? That she was delirious again?

"But— But—" she stammered. "I heard them. Ah Cheng and her husband. Planning a wedding."

Thorpe chuckled, his free hand stroking her hair. "Ah Cheng's been dying to put up your hair. She knew almost before I did that I love you."

"But—but you were so—"

"Nasty?" He chuckled again, then sobered. "My poor Jess. What I put you through. And all because I didn't want to love you." He looked down into her eyes. "You see, love has always been very painful for me. My parents loved each other, I'm sure. But they fought all the time. And they were very busy with little time for me. And no matter how much I loved Ah Cheng I could not *be* the child she had lost."

He sighed. "I guess the real turning point came the day I found my dog dead. Buster was old and ready to go. But I didn't care about that." His arms tightened around her. "It was that day that I decided not to love again. It was simply too painful. And I stuck by my decision all these years. Haviland is nothing. An old childhood friend, hardly a woman."

"And Helen Cheong?" Jess forced herself to ask.

"She's a woman, all right. But a man doesn't marry a woman like that."

He felt her stiffen. "No, my silly kitten. Not because she's Eurasian or even because of her way of life. But because in spite of that gorgeous body, she's just as cold and empty inside as Haviland. A man has needs— even if he determines never to love. But if he's smart, he won't risk satisfying those needs with someone who might love him—and get hurt. I took them both off privately and told them that I was going to marry you. They both know the score now."

Jess trembled in his arms. How could this really be happening? "What—what did they say?"

Thorpe chuckled. "Haviland took it like a trouper. Wished me happiness and all that. Stiff upper lip. Ten minutes later she was shining up to a replacement."

"And Helen?"

Derek's arm tightened around her. "First she made a last grand attempt to win me back, and then she practically spit in my face."

"Oh," said Jess in a small voice.

"It shouldn't have been much of a surprise to her," he explained. "I haven't been to her place since before you and I left for Sabah."

Jess sighed. Everything seemed perfect now. And then she remembered. "What about my room?"

He stared at her. "It's a guest room."

She was glad the darkness hid some of her confusion. "But it looks like— Women—"

He squeezed her. "My reputation with women is largely unearned."

Jess sighed in relief.

"Women *are* fond of chasing me," he said with a smile. "And the nastier I am the more they fall at my feet." He kissed her forehead. "Until I met you, hot and tired, a spunky little kitten daring to act the tiger."

He kissed the tip of her nose. "I knew that you were different, but I wouldn't admit it."

Shuddering, he clasped her to him. "And in the jungle— Dear God, I thought for a while that I'd lose you."

Jess snuggled against him. "But you didn't say— And you've been so—different."

"That's why I held the party—to get you to stay longer. I couldn't bear losing you. But when they went to make the announcement about the new pitcher, you were gone."

Jess stirred in his arms. "What's so important about that? They'll call it Nepenthes Thorpeana or something like that. Won't they?"

Thorpe shook his head. "No, they won't. They'll call it Nepenthes Harringtonia."

For a moment she was silent and then Jess raised her delighted face to his. "Oh, Derek, how wonderful. I'm so proud of you."

He raised an eyebrow. "What's to be proud of? Dick found it."

"Yes, but—"

"No buts," he said, pressing her close. "Out there in the jungle I found something far more important than a new species of plant. I found you."

She burrowed against his chest. "Oh, Derek. I love you. I love you so much."

She felt his arms tighten still more. "I thought you'd never say it. But come on, we've got to find Ah Cheng."

"What for?"

"So she can finalize plans for the wedding," he said with a grin. He brushed her curls lightly with his lips. "But don't let her talk you into a red dress. I want my bride in the white gown she deserves."

Jess grinned back at him, her heart pounding with happiness. "And shall I come to you in a red sedan chair?"

"I don't think I want to kick any door that has you behind it," he replied. "Not as long as you let me in."

Happiness bubbled out of Jess in gay laughter. "There's only one thing I insist on," she said.

She saw his eyes sober as he asked, "Yes, what is it?"

"You must be yourself again," she cried. "Dear Derek, I can't stand it when you're so insufferably polite."

The smile returned to his eyes. "All right, kitten. I'll be my old terrible self."

"Good. After all, that's the man I love."

And, holding hands, they moved off toward the kitchen to let Ah Cheng be the first to hear the good news.

# Silhouette Romance

## IT'S YOUR OWN SPECIAL TIME

*Contemporary romances for today's women.*
*Each month, six very special love stories will be yours*
*from SILHOUETTE. Look for them wherever books are sold*
*or order now from the coupon below.*

### $1.50 each

---

**SILHOUETTE BOOKS**, Department SB/1
1230 Avenue of the Americas
New York, NY 10020

Please send me the books I have checked above. I am enclosing
$_____ (please add 50¢ to cover postage and handling. NYS and
NYC residents please add appropriate sales tax). Send check or
money order—no cash or C.O.D.'s please. Allow six weeks for delivery.

NAME_____

ADDRESS_____

CITY_____ STATE/ZIP_____

# READERS' COMMENTS ON SILHOUETTE ROMANCES:

"Your books are written with so much feeling and quality that they make you feel as if you are part of the story."
—D.C.*, Piedmont, SC

"I'm very particular about the types of romances I read; yours more than fill my thirst for reading."
—C.D., Oxford, MI

"I hope Silhouette novels stay around for many years to come. . . . Keep up the good work."
—P.C., Frederick, MD

"What a relief to be able to escape in a well-written romantic story."
—E.N.. Santa Maria, CA

"Silhouette Romances . . . Fantastic!"
—M.D., Bell, CA

"I'm pleased to be adding your books to my collection—my library is growing in size every day."
—B.L., La Crescenta, CA